CHARLES DICKENS

OLIVER TWIST

ABRIDGED BY

TOBY FORWARD

ILLUSTRATED BY

IASSEN GHIUSELEV

WALKER BOOKS
AND SUBSIDIARIES
LONDON • BOSTON • SYDNEY • AUCKLAND

Introduction

Oliver Twist changed the law, but it didn't change the world. The years following its publication saw a series of Acts of Parliament which attempted, and to some degree succeeded, in improving conditions for children and young people. But there has not been a single year since its publication in 1838 when children have not been victims of parental neglect, criminal exploitation, bureaucratic incompetence, poverty, bullying and abuse. *Oliver Twist* is a book for today, just as much as it was for 1838.

As always with Dickens, the book is a mixture of a serious social issue and a really great read. It's an adventure story of a young boy running away from the workhouse and getting lost in London. It's a revenge story, a mystery, a "buddy" story, a comedy, a thriller and a crime novel. It's also a great cliffhanger, with chapters ending just at a moment when something is about to happen. You'll want to turn the pages.

Dickens is famously sprawling in his story telling. Characters and descriptions of scenes are allowed a lot of space. Surely, there would be pages and pages I could cut and it wouldn't affect the book at all? There must be whole long sections which could skilfully be reduced to a few lines, without any damage to the plot or the atmosphere? Actually, it would probably improve the book to cut it a little, to make it leaner, swifter? No such luck. My admiration for Dickens, already great, grew as I tried to find ways of making the book shorter.

Our principle in this abridgement was that the words of Dickens and only those words should be used. No new sections. No newly-written linking passages. Nothing that wasn't in the original. Which meant I could cut, but not add.

Apart from changing one chapter title, I broke the rule about changing the text in one case only. There was a problem with Fagin. Once he

Charles Dickens

OLIVER TWIST

abridged by Toby Forward

illustrated by Iassen Ghiuselev

SHOEMAKER

has been introduced to the reader, Fagin is hardly ever referred to as anything but "the Jew". In fact, no connection is made between the evil in his character and his being a Jew. There's no link. He doesn't do bad things because he's a Jew. Other bad characters (and Monks is much worse) aren't Jews. It's Bill Sikes who is by far the nastiest character in the book, and he's not Jewish. Yet, despite all that, the simple repetition of the word "Jew" instead of a name or a pronoun is, to a modern reader, offensive. For this reason nearly every instance of the word has been changed to read "him", "his", "Fagin" or some alternative. A few are left in, to make the point that he is a Jew. There seemed to be nothing wrong in that. But the thousands of times the word was used made it more important than it is and it unbalanced the book. So the change was made. Some readers will think this is squeamish. Some will think it hasn't been taken far enough, and it would be a better book for a modern young reader if Fagin the Jew could just be Fagin the villain. *Oliver Twist* is about many things. Anti-Semitism isn't one of them, so in this abridgement, Fagin is incidentally a Jew, it is not the single thing the reader needs to know about him. Language changes circumstances. Circumstances change language. A lot has happened since 1838.

Other than that. This is a slimmer version of a great book. All the characters are here – the Artful Dodger, Nancy, the Bumbles, Fagin, Bill Sikes, Mr Brownlow, Bulls'-eye, Monks. Something will have been lost, but I hope nothing essential. I hope that, being slimmer, it will be attractive to some readers who would not otherwise have given it a try. Trying it, I hope they will enjoy it so much that they will go on to read other great big fat books by Dickens.

Toby Forward
Liverpool, September 2011

CHAPTER

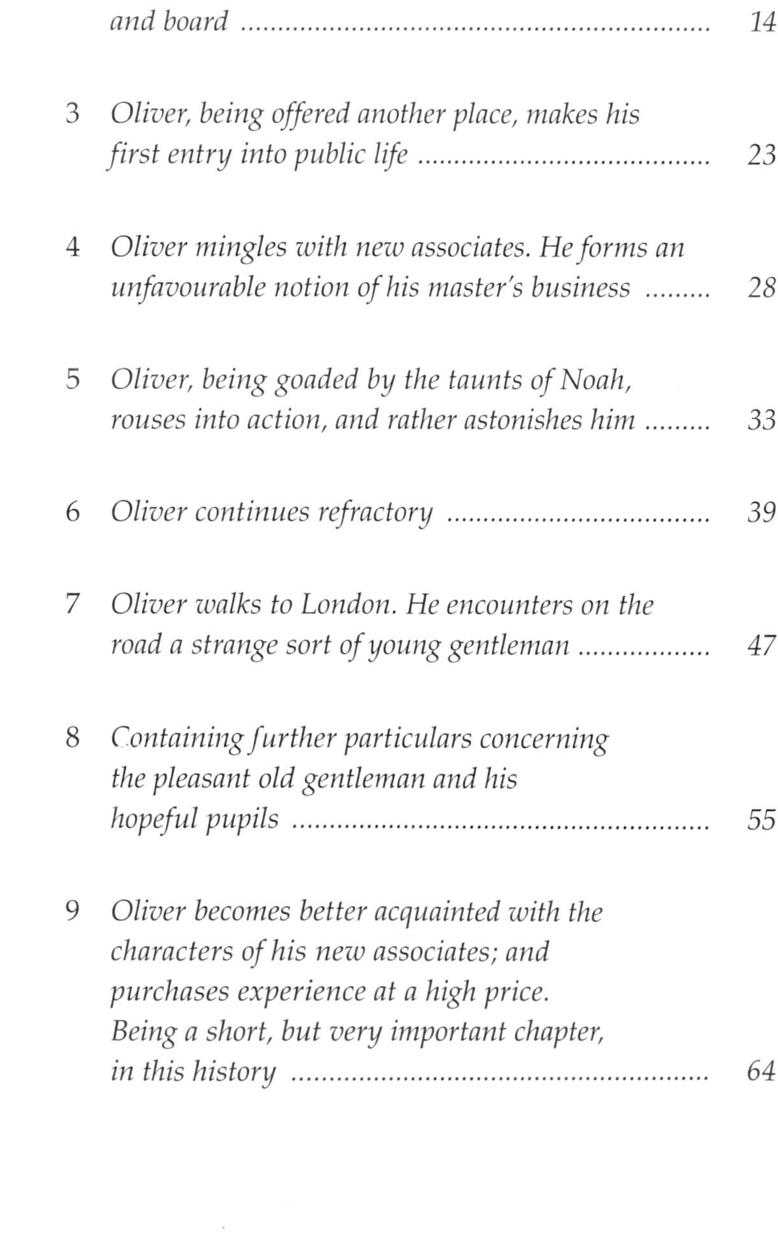

CHAPTER

CHAPTER 1

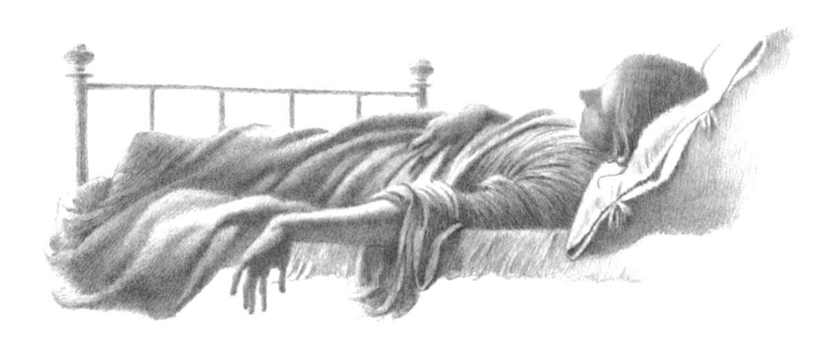

TREATS OF THE PLACE WHERE OLIVER TWIST WAS BORN, AND OF THE CIRCUMSTANCES ATTENDING HIS BIRTH

Among other public buildings in a certain town, which for many reasons it will be prudent to refrain from mentioning, and to which I will assign no fictitious name, there is one anciently common to most towns, great or small: to wit, a workhouse; and in this workhouse was born; on a day and date which I need not trouble myself to repeat, inasmuch as it can be of no possible consequence to the reader, in this stage of the business at all events; the item of mortality whose name is prefixed to the head of this chapter.

The fact is, that there was considerable difficulty in inducing Oliver to take upon himself the office of respiration – a troublesome practice, but one which custom has rendered necessary to our easy existence; and for some time he lay gasping on a little flock mattress, rather unequally poised between this world and the next: the balance being decidedly in favour of the latter.

Oliver and Nature fought out the point between them. The result was, that, after a few struggles, Oliver breathed, sneezed, and proceeded to advertise to the inmates of the workhouse the fact of a new burden having been imposed upon the parish.

As Oliver gave this first proof of the free and proper action of his lungs, the patchwork coverlet which was carelessly flung over the iron bedstead, rustled; the pale face of a young woman was raised feebly from the pillow; and a faint voice imperfectly articulated the words, "Let me see the child, and die."

The surgeon deposited it in her arms. She imprinted her cold white lips passionately on its forehead; passed her hands over her face; gazed wildly round; shuddered; fell back – and died. They chafed her breast, hands and temples; but the blood had stopped for ever. They talked of hope and comfort. They had been strangers too long.

"It's all over, Mrs Thingummy!" said the surgeon at last.

"She was brought here last night," replied the old woman, "by the overseer's order. She was found lying in the street. She had walked some distance, for her shoes were worn to pieces; but where she came from, or where she was going to, nobody knows."

The surgeon leaned over the body, and raised the left hand. "The old story," he said, shaking his head: "no wedding ring, I see. Ah! Goodnight!"

Oliver cried lustily. If he could have known that he was an orphan, left to the tender mercies of churchwardens and overseers, perhaps he would have cried the louder.

CHAPTER 2

TREATS OF OLIVER TWIST'S GROWTH, EDUCATION AND BOARD

Oliver Twist's ninth birthday found him a pale thin child, somewhat diminutive in stature, and decidedly small in circumference. But nature or inheritance had implanted a good sturdy spirit in Oliver's breast. It had had plenty of room to expand, thanks to the spare diet of the establishment; and perhaps to this circumstance may be attributed his having any ninth birthday at all. Be this as it may, however, it *was* his ninth birthday; and he was keeping it in the coal-cellar with a select party of two other young gentlemen, who, after participating with him in a sound thrashing, had been locked up for atrociously presuming to be hungry, when Mrs Mann, the good lady of the house, was unexpectedly startled by the apparition of Mr Bumble, the beadle, striving to undo the wicket of the garden-gate.

"Goodness gracious! Is that you, Mr Bumble, sir?" said Mrs Mann.

"Do you think this respectful or proper conduct, Mrs Mann," inquired Mr Bumble, grasping his cane, "to keep the parish officers a waiting at your garden-gate, when they come here upon porochial business with the porochial orphans? Are you aweer, Mrs Mann, that you are, as I may say, a porochial delegate, and a stipendiary?"

"I'm sure, Mr Bumble, that I was only a telling one or two of the dear children as is so fond of you, that it was you a coming," replied Mrs Mann with great humility.

Mrs Mann ushered the beadle into a small parlour with a brick floor; placed a seat for him; and officiously deposited his cocked hat and cane on the table before him. Mr Bumble wiped from his forehead the perspiration which his walk had engendered, glanced complacently at the cocked hat, and smiled. Yes, he smiled. Beadles are but men; and Mr Bumble smiled.

"And now about business," said the beadle, taking out a leathern pocket-book. "The child that was half-baptized Oliver Twist, is nine year old today."

"Bless him!" interposed Mrs Mann, inflaming her left eye with the corner of her apron.

"And notwithstanding a offered reward of ten pound, which was afterwards increased to twenty pound. Notwithstanding the most superlative, and, I may say, supernat'ral exertions on the part of this parish," said Bumble, "we have never been able to discover who is his father, or what was his mother's settlement, name, or condition."

Mrs Mann raised her hands in astonishment; but added, after a moment's reflection, "How comes he to have any name at all, then?"

The beadle drew himself up with great pride, and said, "I inwented it."

"You, Mr Bumble!"

"I, Mrs Mann. We name our fondlings in alphabetical order. The last was a S, – Swubble, I named him. This was a T, – Twist, I named *him*. The next one as comes will be Unwin, and the next Vilkins. I have got names ready made to the end of the alphabet, and all the way through it again, when we come to Z."

"Why, you're quite a literary character, sir!" said Mrs Mann.

"Well, well," said the beadle, evidently gratified with the compliment; "perhaps I may be. Perhaps I may be, Mrs Mann." He finished the gin-and-water, and added, "Oliver being now too old to remain here, the board have determined to have him back into the house. I have come out myself to take him there. So let me see him at once."

"I'll fetch him directly," said Mrs Mann, leaving the room for that purpose. Oliver, having had as much of the outer coat of dirt, which encrusted his face and hands, removed, as could be scrubbed off in one washing by this time, was led into the room by his benevolent protectress.

"Make a bow to the gentleman, Oliver," said Mrs Mann.

Oliver made a bow, which was divided between the beadle on the chair, and the cocked hat on the table.

"Will you go along with me, Oliver?" said Mr Bumble, in a majestic voice.

Oliver was about to say that he would go along with anybody with great readiness, when, glancing upward, he caught sight of Mrs Mann, who had got behind the beadle's chair, and was shaking her fist at him with a furious countenance. He took the hint at once, for the fist had been too often impressed upon his body not to be deeply impressed upon his recollection.

"Will *she* go with me?" inquired poor Oliver.

"No, she can't," replied Mr Bumble. "But she'll come and see you sometimes."

This was no very great consolation to the child. Young as he was, however, he had sense enough to make a feint of feeling great regret at going away. It was no very difficult matter for the boy to call tears into his eyes. Hunger and recent ill-usage are great assistants if you want to cry; and Oliver cried very naturally indeed. Mrs Mann gave him a thousand embraces, and, what Oliver wanted a great deal more, a piece of bread and butter, lest he should seem too hungry when he got to the workhouse. With the slice of bread in his hand, and the little brown-cloth parish cap on his head, Oliver was then led away by Mr Bumble from the wretched home where one kind word or look had never lighted the gloom of his infant years. And yet he burst into an agony of childish grief, as the cottage-gate closed after him. Wretched as were the little companions in misery he was leaving behind, they were the only friends he had ever known; and a sense of his loneliness in the great wide world, sank into the child's heart for the first time.

Oliver had not been within the walls of the workhouse a quarter of an hour, and had scarcely completed the demolition of a second slice of bread, when Mr Bumble, who had handed him over to the care of an old woman, returned; and, telling him it was a board night, informed him that the board had said he was to appear before it forthwith.

Not having a very clearly defined notion of what a live board was, Oliver was rather astounded by this intelligence, and was not quite certain whether he ought to laugh or cry. He had no time to think about the matter, however; for Mr Bumble gave him a tap on the head, with his cane, to wake him up: and another on the back to make him lively: and bidding him follow, conducted him into a large white-washed room, where eight or ten fat gentlemen were sitting round a table. At the top of the table, seated in an armchair rather higher than the rest, was a particularly fat gentleman with a very round, red face.

"Bow to the board," said Bumble. Oliver brushed away two or three tears that were lingering in his eyes; and seeing no board but the table, fortunately bowed to that.

"What's your name, boy?" said the gentleman in the high chair.

Oliver was frightened at the sight of so many gentlemen, which made him tremble: and the beadle gave him another tap behind, which made him cry. These two causes made him answer in a very low and hesitating voice; whereupon a gentleman in a white waistcoat said he was a fool. Which was a capital way of raising his spirits, and putting him quite at his ease.

"Boy," said the gentleman in the high chair, "listen to me. You know you're an orphan, I suppose?"

"What's that, sir?" inquired poor Oliver.

"The boy *is* a fool – I thought he was," said the gentleman in the white waistcoat.

"Well! You have come here to be educated, and taught a useful trade," said the red-faced gentleman in the high chair.

"So you'll begin to pick oakum tomorrow morning at six o'clock," added the surly one in the white waistcoat.

For the combination of both these blessings in the one simple process of picking oakum, Oliver bowed low by the direction of the beadle, and was then hurried away to a large ward: where, on a rough, hard bed, he sobbed himself to sleep. What a noble illustration of the tender laws of England! They let the paupers go to sleep!

The room in which the boys were fed, was a large stone hall, with a copper at one end: out of which the master, dressed in an apron for the purpose, and assisted by one or two women, ladled the gruel at mealtimes. Of this festive composition each boy had one porringer, and no more – except on occasions of great public rejoicing, when he had two ounces and a quarter of bread besides. The bowls never wanted washing. The boys polished them with their spoons till they shone again; and when they had performed this operation (which never took very long, the spoons being nearly as large as the bowls), they would sit staring at the copper, with such eager eyes, as if they could have devoured the very bricks of which it was composed; employing themselves, meanwhile, in sucking their fingers most assiduously, with the view of catching up any stray splashes of gruel that might have been cast thereon. Boys have generally excellent appetites. Oliver Twist and his companions suffered the tortures of slow starvation for three months: at last they got so voracious and wild with hunger, that one boy, who was tall for his age, and hadn't been used

to that sort of thing (for his father had kept a small cook-shop), hinted darkly to his companions, that unless he had another basin of gruel *per diem*, he was afraid he might some night happen to eat the boy who slept next him, who happened to be a weakly youth of tender age. He had a wild, hungry eye; and they implicitly believed him. A council was held; lots were cast who should walk up to the master after supper that evening, and ask for more; and it fell to Oliver Twist.

The evening arrived; the boys took their places. The master, in his cook's uniform, stationed himself at the copper; his pauper assistants ranged themselves behind him; the gruel was served out; and a long grace was said over the short commons. The gruel disappeared; the boys whispered each other, and winked at Oliver; while his next neighbours nudged him. Child as he was, he was desperate with hunger, and reckless with misery. He rose from the table; and advancing to the master, basin and spoon in hand, said: somewhat alarmed at his own temerity:

"Please, sir, I want some more."

The master was a fat, healthy man; but he turned very pale. He gazed in stupefied astonishment on the small rebel for some seconds, and then clung for support to the copper. The assistants were paralyzed with wonder; the boys with fear.

"What!" said the master at length, in a faint voice.

"Please, sir," replied Oliver, "I want some more."

The master aimed a blow at Oliver's head with the ladle; pinioned him in his arms; and shrieked aloud for the beadle.

The board were sitting in solemn conclave, when Mr Bumble rushed into the room in great excitement, and addressing the gentleman in the high chair, said,

"Mr Limbkins, I beg your pardon, sir! Oliver Twist has asked for more!"

There was a general start. Horror was depicted on every countenance.

"For *more*!" said Mr Limbkins. "Compose yourself, Bumble, and answer me distinctly. Do I understand that he asked for more, after he had eaten the supper allotted by the dietary?"

"He did, sir," replied Bumble.

"That boy will be hung," said the gentleman in the white waistcoat. "I know that boy will be hung."

Nobody controverted the prophetic gentleman's opinion. An animated discussion took place. Oliver was ordered into instant confinement; and a bill was next morning pasted on the outside of the gate, offering a reward of five pounds to anybody who would take Oliver Twist off the hands of the parish. In other words, five pounds and Oliver Twist were offered to any man or woman who wanted an apprentice to any trade, business, or calling.

"I never was more convinced of anything in my life," said the gentleman in the white waistcoat, as he knocked at the gate and read the bill next morning: "I never was more convinced of anything in my life, than I am that that boy will come to be hung."

CHAPTER 3

OLIVER, BEING OFFERED ANOTHER PLACE, MAKES HIS FIRST ENTRY INTO PUBLIC LIFE

Mr Bumble had been despatched to make various preliminary inquiries, with the view of finding out some captain or other who wanted a cabin-boy without any friends; and was returning to the workhouse to communicate the result of his mission; when he encountered at the gate, no less a person than Mr Sowerberry, the parochial undertaker.

Mr Sowerberry, was a tall, gaunt, large-jointed man, attired in a suit of threadbare black, with darned cotton stockings of the same colour, and shoes to answer. His features were not naturally intended to wear a smiling aspect, but he was in general rather given to professional jocosity. His step was elastic, and his face betokened inward pleasantry, as he advanced to Mr Bumble, and shook him cordially by the hand.

"By the bye," said Mr Bumble, "you don't know anybody who wants a boy, do you? A porochial 'prentis, who is at present a deadweight; a millstone, as I may say; round the porochial throat? Liberal terms, Mr Sowerberry, liberal terms!" As Mr Bumble spoke, he raised his cane to the bill above him, and gave three distinct raps upon the words "five pounds": which were printed thereon in Roman capitals of a gigantic size.

"Gadso!" said the undertaker: taking Mr Bumble by the gilt-edged lapel of his official coat; "that's just the very thing I wanted to speak to you about."

Mr Bumble grasped the undertaker by the arm, and led him into the building. Mr Sowerberry was closeted with the board for five minutes; and it was arranged that Oliver should go to him that evening "upon liking" – a phrase which means, in the case of a parish apprentice, that if the master find, upon a short trial, that he can get enough work out of a boy without putting too much food into him, he shall have him for a term of years, to do what he likes with.

When little Oliver was taken before "the gentlemen" that evening; and informed that he was to go, that night, as general house-lad to a coffin-maker's; and that if he complained of his situation, or ever came back to the parish again, he would be sent to sea, there to be drowned, or knocked on the head, as the case might be, he evinced so little emotion, that they by common consent pronounced him a hardened young rascal, and ordered Mr Bumble to remove him forthwith.

The undertaker, who had just put up the shutters of his shop, was making some entries in his day-book by the light of a most appropriate dismal candle, when Mr Bumble entered.

"Aha!" said the undertaker: looking up from the book, and pausing in the middle of a word; "is that you, Bumble?"

"No one else, Mr Sowerberry," replied the beadle. "Here! I've brought the boy." Oliver made a bow.

"Oh! that's the boy, is it?" said the undertaker: raising the candle above his head, to get a better view of Oliver. "Mrs Sowerberry, will you have the goodness to come here a moment, my dear?"

Mrs Sowerberry emerged from a little room behind the shop, and presented the form of a short, thin, squeezed-up woman, with a vixenish countenance.

"My dear," said Mr Sowerberry, deferentially, "this is the boy from the workhouse that I told you of." Oliver bowed again.

"Dear me!" said the undertaker's wife, "he's very small."

"Why, he *is* rather small," replied Mr Bumble: looking at Oliver as if it were his fault that he was no bigger; "he *is* small. There's no denying it. But he'll grow, Mrs Sowerberry – he'll grow."

"Ah! I dare say he will," replied the lady pettishly, "on our victuals and our drink. I see no saving in parish children, not I; for they always cost more to keep, than they're worth. However, men always think they know best. There! Get downstairs, little bag o' bones." With this, the undertaker's wife opened a side door, and pushed Oliver down a steep flight of stairs into a stone cell, damp and dark: forming the ante-room to the coal-cellar, and denominated "kitchen"; wherein sat a slatternly girl, in shoes down at heel, and blue worsted stockings very much out of repair.

"Here, Charlotte," said Mrs Sowerberry, who had followed Oliver down, "give this boy some of the cold bits that were put by for Trip. He hasn't come home since the morning, so he may go without 'em. I dare say the boy isn't too dainty to eat 'em – are you, boy?"

Oliver, whose eyes had glistened at the mention of meat, and who was trembling with eagerness to devour it, replied in the negative; and a plateful of coarse broken victuals was set before him.

"Well," said the undertaker's wife, when Oliver had finished his supper: which she had regarded in silent horror, and with fearful auguries of his future appetite: "have you done?"

There being nothing eatable within his reach, Oliver replied in the affirmative.

"Then come with me," said Mrs Sowerberry: taking up a dim and dirty lamp, and leading the way upstairs; "your bed's under the counter. You don't mind sleeping among the coffins, I suppose? But it doesn't much matter whether you do or don't, for you can't sleep anywhere else. Come; don't keep me here all night!"

Oliver lingered no longer, but meekly followed his new mistress.

CHAPTER 4

OLIVER MINGLES WITH NEW ASSOCIATES. HE FORMS AN UNFAVOURABLE NOTION OF HIS MASTER'S BUSINESS

Oliver, being left to himself in the undertaker's shop, set the lamp down on a workman's bench, and gazed timidly about him with a feeling of awe and dread, which many people a good deal older than he, will be at no loss to understand. An unfinished coffin on black trestles, which stood in the middle of the shop, looked so gloomy and death-like that a cold tremble came over him, every time his eyes wandered in the direction of the dismal object: from which he almost expected to see some frightful form slowly rear its head, to drive him mad with terror. Against the wall were ranged, in regular array, a long row of elm boards cut in the same shape: looking in the dim light like high-shouldered ghosts with their hands in their breeches pockets. Coffin-plates, elm-chips, bright-headed nails, and shreds of black cloth, lay scattered on the floor; and the wall behind the counter was ornamented with a lively representation of two mutes in very stiff neckcloths, on duty at a large private door, with a hearse drawn by four black steeds, approaching in the distance. The shop was close and hot. The atmosphere seemed tainted with the smell of coffins. The recess beneath the counter in which his flock mattress was thrust looked like a grave.

Oliver was awakened in the morning, by a loud kicking at the outside of the shop-door: which, before he could huddle on his clothes, was repeated, in an angry and impetuous manner, about twenty-five times. When he began to undo the chain, the legs desisted, and a voice began.

"Open the door, will yer?" cried the voice which belonged to the legs which had kicked at the door.

"I will, directly, sir," replied Oliver: undoing the chain, and turning the key.

"I suppose yer the new boy, ain't yer?" said the voice through the keyhole.

"Yes, sir," replied Oliver.

"How old are yer?" inquired the voice.

"Ten, sir," replied Oliver.

"Then I'll whop yer when I get in," said the voice; "you just see if I don't, that's all, my work'us brat!" and having made this obliging promise, the voice began to whistle.

Oliver had been too often subjected to the process to which the very expressive monosyllable just recorded bears reference, to entertain the smallest doubt that the owner of the voice, whoever he might be, would redeem his pledge, most honourably. He drew back the bolts with a trembling hand, and opened the door.

For a second or two, Oliver glanced up the street, and down the street, and over the way: impressed with the belief that the unknown, who had addressed him through the keyhole, had walked a few paces off, to warm himself; for nobody did he see but a big charity-boy, sitting on a post in front of the house, eating a slice of bread and butter: which he cut into wedges, the size of his mouth, with a clasp knife, and then consumed with great dexterity.

"I beg your pardon, sir," said Oliver at length: seeing that no other visitor made his appearance: "did you knock?"

"I kicked," replied the charity-boy.

"Did you want a coffin, sir?" inquired Oliver, innocently.

At this the charity-boy looked monstrous fierce; and said that Oliver would want one before long, if he cut jokes with his superiors in that way.

"Yer don't know who I am, I suppose, Work'us?" said the charity-boy, in continuation: descending from the top of the post, meanwhile, with edifying gravity.

"No, sir," rejoined Oliver.

"I'm Mister Noah Claypole," said the charity-boy, "and you're under me.

Take down the shutters, yer idle young ruffian!" With this, Mr Claypole administered a kick to Oliver, and entered the shop with a dignified air, which did him great credit. It is difficult for a large-headed, small-eyed youth, of lumbering make and heavy countenance, to look dignified under any circumstances; but it is more especially so, when superadded to these personal attractions are a red nose and yellow smalls.

Oliver, having taken down the shutters, and broken a pane of glass in his effort to stagger away beneath the weight of the first one to a small court at the side of the house in which they were kept during the day, was graciously assisted by Noah: who having consoled him with the assurance that "he'd catch it," condescended to help him. Mr Sowerberry came down soon after. Shortly afterwards, Mrs Sowerberry appeared. Oliver having "caught it," in fulfilment of Noah's prediction, followed that young gentleman down the stairs to breakfast.

"Come near the fire, Noah," said Charlotte. "I saved a nice little bit of bacon for you from master's breakfast. Oliver, shut that door at Mister Noah's back, and take them bits that I've put out on the cover of the bread-pan. There's your tea; take it away to that box, and drink it there, and make haste, for they'll want you to mind the shop. D'ye hear?"

"D'ye hear, Work'us?" said Noah Claypole.

"Lor, Noah!" said Charlotte, "what a rum creature you are! Why don't you let the boy alone?"

"Let him alone!" said Noah. "Why everybody lets him alone enough, for the matter of that. Neither his father nor his mother will ever interfere with him. All his relations let him have his own way pretty well. Eh, Charlotte? He! he! he!"

"Oh, you queer soul!" said Charlotte, bursting into a hearty laugh, in which she was joined by Noah; after which they both looked scornfully at poor Oliver Twist, as he sat shivering on the box in the coldest corner of the room, and ate the stale pieces which had been specially reserved for him.

Noah was a charity-boy, but not a workhouse orphan. No chance-child was he, for he could trace his genealogy all the way back to his parents, who lived hard by; his mother being a washerwoman, and his father a drunken soldier, discharged with a wooden leg, and a diurnal pension of twopence-halfpenny and an unstateable fraction. The shop-boys in the neighbourhood had long been in the habit of branding Noah, in the public streets, with the ignominious epithets of "leathers," "charity," and the like; and Noah had borne them without reply. But, now that fortune had cast in his way a nameless orphan, at whom even the meanest could point the finger of scorn, he retorted on him with interest. This affords charming food for contemplation. It shows us what a beautiful thing human nature may be made to be; and how impartially the same amiable qualities are developed in the finest lord and the dirtiest charity-boy.

CHAPTER 5

OLIVER, BEING GOADED BY THE TAUNTS OF NOAH, ROUSES INTO ACTION, AND RATHER ASTONISHES HIM

The month's trial over, Oliver was formally apprenticed. It was a nice sickly season just at this time. In commercial phrase, coffins were looking up; and, in the course of a few weeks, Oliver acquired a great deal of experience.

And now I come to a very important passage in Oliver's history; for I have to record an act, slight and unimportant perhaps in appearance, but which indirectly produced a material change in all his future prospects and proceedings.

One day, Oliver and Noah had descended into the kitchen at the usual dinner-hour, to banquet upon a small joint of mutton – a pound and a half of the worst end of the neck – when Charlotte being called out of the way, there ensued a brief interval of time, which Noah Claypole, being hungry and vicious, considered he could not possibly devote to a worthier purpose than aggravating and tantalizing young Oliver Twist.

Intent upon this innocent amusement, Noah put his feet on the table-cloth; and pulled Oliver's hair; and twitched his ears; and expressed his opinion that he was a "sneak"; and furthermore announced his intention of coming to see him hanged, whenever that desirable event should take place; and entered upon various topics of petty annoyance, like a malicious and ill-conditioned charity-boy as he was. But none of these taunts producing the desired effect of making Oliver cry, Noah attempted to be more facetious still; and in this attempt, did what many small wits sometimes do to this day, when they want to be funny. He got rather personal.

"Work'us," said Noah, "how's your mother?"

"She's dead," replied Oliver; "don't you say anything about her to me!"

Oliver's colour rose as he said this; he breathed quickly; and there was a curious working of the mouth and nostrils, which Mr Claypole thought must be the immediate precursor of a violent fit of crying. Under this impression he returned to the charge.

"What did she die of, Work'us?" said Noah.

"Of a broken heart, some of our old nurses told me," replied Oliver: more as if he were talking to himself, than answering Noah. "I think I know what it must be to die of that."

"Tol de rol lol lol, right fol lairy, Work'us," said Noah, as a tear rolled down Oliver's cheek. "What's set you a snivelling now?"

"Not *you*," replied Oliver, sharply. "There; that's enough. Don't say anything more to me about her; you'd better not!"

"Better not!" exclaimed Noah. "Well! Better not! Work'us, don't be impudent. *Your* mother, too! She was a nice 'un, she was. Oh, Lor!" And here, Noah nodded his head expressively; and curled up as much of his small red nose as muscular action could collect together, for the occasion.

"Yer know, Work'us," continued Noah, emboldened by Oliver's silence, and speaking in a jeering tone of affected pity: of all tones the most annoying: "Yer know, Work'us, it can't be helped now; and of course yer couldn't help it then; and I'm very sorry for it; and I'm sure we all are, and pity yer very much. But yer must know, Work'us, yer mother was a regular right-down bad 'un."

"What did you say?" inquired Oliver, looking up very quickly.

"A regular right-down bad 'un, Work'us," replied Noah, coolly. "And it's a great deal better, Work'us, that she died when she did, or else she'd have been hard labouring in Bridewell, or transported, or hung; which is more likely than either, isn't it?"

Crimson with fury, Oliver started up, overthrew the chair and table; seized Noah by the throat; shook him, in the violence of his rage, till his teeth chattered in his head; and, collecting his whole force into one heavy blow, felled him to the ground.

A minute ago, the boy had looked the quiet, mild, dejected creature that harsh treatment had made him. But his spirit was roused at last; the cruel insult to his dead mother had set his blood on fire. His breast heaved; his attitude was erect; his eye bright and vivid; his whole person changed, as he stood glaring over the cowardly tormentor who now lay crouching at his feet; and defied him with an energy he had never known before.

"He'll murder me!" blubbered Noah. "Charlotte! missis! Here's the new

boy a murdering of me! Help! help! Oliver's gone mad! Char–lotte!"

Noah's shouts were responded to, by a loud scream from Charlotte, and a louder from Mrs Sowerberry; the former of whom rushed into the kitchen by a side-door, while the latter paused on the staircase till she was quite certain that it was consistent with the preservation of human life, to come further down.

"Oh, you little wretch!" screamed Charlotte: seizing Oliver with her utmost force, which was about equal to that of a moderately strong man in particularly good training, "Oh, you little un-grate-ful, mur-de-rous, hor-rid villain!" And between every syllable, Charlotte gave Oliver a blow with all her might: accompanying it with a scream, for the benefit of society.

Charlotte's fist was by no means a light one; but, lest it should not be effectual in calming Oliver's wrath, Mrs Sowerberry plunged into the kitchen, and assisted to hold him with one hand, while she scratched his face with the other. In his favourable position of affairs, Noah rose from the ground, and pommelled him behind.

This was rather too violent exercise to last long. When they were all wearied out, and could tear and beat no longer, they dragged Oliver, struggling and shouting, but nothing daunted, into the dust-cellar, and there locked him up. This being done, Mrs Sowerberry sunk into a chair, and burst into tears.

"Bless her, she's going off!" said Charlotte. "A glass of water, Noah, dear. Make haste!"

"Oh! Charlotte," said Mrs Sowerberry; speaking as well as she could, through a deficiency of breath, and a sufficiency of cold water, which Noah had poured over her head and shoulders. "Oh! Charlotte, what a mercy we have not all been murdered in our beds!"

"Ah! mercy indeed, ma'am," was the reply. "I only hope this'll teach master not to have any more of these dreadful creatures, that are born to be murderers and robbers from their very cradle. Poor Noah! He was all but killed, ma'am, when I come in."

"Poor fellow!" said Mrs Sowerberry: looking piteously on the charity-boy.

Noah, whose top waistcoat-button might have been somewhere on a level with the crown of Oliver's head, rubbed his eyes with the inside of his wrists while this commiseration was bestowed upon him, and performed some affecting tears and sniffs.

"What's to be done!" exclaimed Mrs Sowerberry. "Your master's not at home; there's not a man in the house, and he'll kick that door down in ten minutes." Oliver's vigorous plunges against the bit of timber in question rendered this occurance highly probable.

"Dear, dear! I don't know, ma'am," said Charlotte, "unless we send for the police officers."

"Or the millingtary," suggested Mr Claypole.

"No, no," said Mrs Sowerberry: bethinking herself of Oliver's old friend. "Run to Mr Bumble, Noah, and tell him to come here directly, and not to lose a minute; never mind your cap! Make haste! You can hold a knife to that black eye, as you run along. It'll keep the swelling down."

Noah stopped to make no reply, but started off at his fullest speed; and very much it astonished the people who were out walking, to see a charity-boy tearing through the streets pell-mell, with no cap on his head, and a clasp-knife at his eye.

CHAPTER 6

OLIVER CONTINUES REFRACTORY

Noah Claypole ran along the streets at his swiftest pace, and paused not once for breath, until he reached the workhouse-gate. Having rested here, for a minute or so, to collect a good burst of sobs and an imposing show of tears and terror, he knocked loudly at the wicket; and presented such a rueful face to the aged pauper who opened it, that even he, who saw nothing but rueful faces about him at the best of times, started back in astonishment.

"Why, what's the matter with the boy!" said the old pauper.

"Mr Bumble! Mr Bumble!" cried Noah, with well-affected dismay: and in tones so loud and agitated, that they not only caught the ear of Mr Bumble himself, who happened to be hard by, but alarmed him so much that he rushed into the yard without his cocked hat – which is a very curious and remarkable circumstance: as showing that even a beadle, acted upon by a sudden and powerful impulse, may be afflicted with a momentary visitation of loss of self-possession, and forgetfulness of personal dignity.

"Oh, Mr Bumble, sir!" said Noah: "Oliver, sir, Oliver has—"

"What? What?" interposed Mr Bumble: with a gleam of pleasure in his metallic eyes. "Not run away; he hasn't run away, has he, Noah?"

"No, sir, no. Not run away, sir, but he's turned wicious," replied Noah. "He tried to murder me, sir; and then he tried to murder Charlotte; and then missis. Oh! what dreadful pain it is! Such agony, please, sir!" And here, Noah writhed and twisted his body into an extensive variety of eel-like positions; thereby giving Mr Bumble to understand that, from the violent and sanguinary onset of Oliver Twist, he had sustained severe internal injury and damage, from which he was at that moment suffering the acutest torture.

When Noah saw that the intelligence he communicated perfectly paralyzed Mr Bumble, he imparted additional effect thereunto, by bewailing his dreadful wounds ten times louder than before; and when he observed a gentleman in a white waistcoat crossing the yard, he was more tragic in his lamentations than ever: rightly conceiving it highly expedient to attract the notice, and rouse the indignation, of the gentleman aforesaid.

The gentleman's notice was very soon attracted; for he had not walked three paces, when he turned angrily round, and inquired what that young cur was howling for, and why Mr Bumble did not favour him with something which would render the series of vocular exclamations so designated, an involuntary process?

"It's a poor boy from the free-school, sir," replied Mr Bumble, "who has been nearly murdered – all but murdered, sir – by young Twist."

"By Jove!" exclaimed the gentleman in the white waistcoat, stopping short. "I knew it! I felt a strange presentiment from the very first, that that audacious young savage would come to be hung!"

"He has likewise attempted, sir, to murder the female servant," said Mr Bumble, with a face of ashy paleness.

"And his missis," interposed Mr Claypole.

"And his master, too, I think you said, Noah?" added Mr Bumble.

"No! he's out, or he would have murdered him," replied Noah. "He said he wanted to."

"Ah! Said he wanted to, did he, my boy?" inquired the gentleman in the white waistcoat.

"Yes, sir," replied Noah. "And please, sir, missis wants to know whether Mr Bumble can spare time to step up there, directly, and flog him – 'cause master's out."

"Certainly, my boy; certainly," said the gentleman in the white waistcoat: smiling benignly, and patting Noah's head, which was about three inches higher than his own. "You're a good boy – a very good boy. Here's a penny for you. Bumble, just step up to Sowerberry's with your cane, and see what's best to be done. Don't spare him, Bumble."

"No, I will not, sir," replied the beadle. And the cocked hat and cane having been, by this time, adjusted to their owner's satisfaction, Mr Bumble and Noah Claypole betook themselves with all speed to the undertaker's shop.

Here the position of affairs had not at all improved. Sowerberry had not yet returned, and Oliver continued to kick, with undiminished vigour, at the cell-door. The accounts of his ferocity, as related by Mrs Sowerberry and Charlotte, were of so startling a nature, that Mr Bumble judged it prudent to parley, before opening the door. With this view he gave a kick at the outside, by way of prelude; and, then, applying his mouth to the keyhole, said, in a deep and impressive tone:

"Oliver!"

"Come; you let me out!" replied Oliver, from the inside.

"Do you know this here voice, Oliver?" said Mr Bumble.

"Yes," replied Oliver.

"Ain't you afraid of it, sir? Ain't you a-trembling while I speak, sir?" said Mr Bumble.

"No!" replied Oliver, boldly.

An answer so different from the one he had expected to elicit, and was in the habit of receiving, staggered Mr Bumble not a little. He stepped back from the keyhole; drew himself up to his full height; and looked from one to another of the three bystanders, in mute astonishment.

"Oh, you know, Mr Bumble, he must be mad," said Mrs Sowerberry. "No boy in half his senses could venture to speak so to you."

"It's not Madness, ma'am," replied Mr Bumble, after a few moments of deep meditation. "It's Meat."

"What?" exclaimed Mrs Sowerberry.

"Meat, ma'am, meat," replied Bumble, with stern emphasis. "You've overfed him, ma'am. You've raised a artificial soul and spirit in him, ma'am, unbecoming a person of his condition: as the board, Mrs Sowerberry, who are practical philosophers, will tell you. What have paupers to do with soul or spirit? It's quite enough that we let 'em have live bodies. If you had kept the boy on gruel, ma'am, this would never have happened."

"Dear, dear!" ejaculated Mrs Sowerberry, piously raising her eyes to the kitchen ceiling: "this comes of being liberal!"

The liberality of Mrs Sowerberry to Oliver, had consisted of a profuse bestowal upon him of all the dirty odds and ends which nobody else would eat; so there was a great deal of meekness and self-devotion in her voluntarily remaining under Mr Bumble's heavy accusation. Of which, to do her justice, she was wholly innocent, in thought, word, or deed.

"Ah!" said Mr Bumble, when the lady brought her eyes down to earth again; "the only thing that can be done now, that I know of, is to leave him in the cellar for a day or so, till he's a little starved down; and then to take him out, and keep him on gruel all through his apprenticeship. He comes of a bad family. Excitable natures, Mrs Sowerberry! Both the nurse and doctor said, that that mother of his made her way here, against difficulties and pain that would have killed any well-disposed woman, weeks before."

At this point of Mr Bumble's discourse, Oliver, just hearing enough to know that some allusion was being made to his mother, recommenced kicking, with a violence that rendered every other sound inaudible. Sowerberry returned at this juncture. Oliver's offence having been explained to him, with such exaggerations as the ladies thought best calculated to rouse his ire, he unlocked the cellar-door in a twinkling, and dragged his rebellious apprentice out, by the collar.

Oliver's clothes had been torn in the beating he had received; his face was bruised and scratched; and his hair scattered over his forehead. The angry flush had not disappeared, however; and when he was pulled out of his prison, he scowled boldly on Noah, and looked quite undismayed.

"Now, you are a nice young fellow, ain't you?" said Sowerberry; giving Oliver a shake, and a box on the ear.

"He called my mother names," replied Oliver.

"Well, and what if he did, you little ungrateful wretch?" said Mrs Sowerberry. "She deserved what he said, and worse."

"She didn't," said Oliver.

"She did," said Mrs Sowerberry.

"It's a lie!" said Oliver.

Mrs Sowerberry burst into a flood of tears.

This flood of tears left Mr Sowerberry no alternative. If he had hesitated for one instant to punish Oliver most severely, it must be quite clear to every experienced reader that he would have been, according to all precedents in disputes of matrimony established, a brute, an unnatural husband, an insulting creature, a base imitation of a man, and various other agreeable characters too numerous for recital within the limits of this chapter. To do him justice, he was, as far as his power went – it was not very extensive – kindly disposed towards the boy; perhaps, because it was his interest to be so; perhaps, because his wife disliked him. The flood of tears, however, left him no resource; so he at once gave him a drubbing, which satisfied even Mrs Sowerberry herself, and rendered Mr Bumble's subsequent application of the parochial cane, rather unnecessary. For the rest of the day, he was shut up in the back kitchen, in company with a pump and a slice of bread; and, at night, Mrs Sowerberry, after making various remarks outside the door, by no means complimentary to the memory of his mother, looked into the room, and, amidst the jeers and pointings of Noah and Charlotte, ordered him upstairs to his dismal bed.

It was not until he was left alone in the silence and stillness of the gloomy workshop of the undertaker, that Oliver gave way to the feelings which the day's treatment may be supposed likely to have awakened in a mere child. He had listened to their taunts with a look of contempt; he

had borne the lash without a cry: for he felt that pride swelling in his heart which would have kept down a shriek to the last, though they had roasted him alive. But now, when there were none to see or hear him, he fell upon his knees on the floor; and, hiding his face in his hands, wept such tears as, God send for the credit of our nature, few so young may ever have cause to pour out before him!

For a long time, Oliver remained motionless in this attitude. The candle was burning low in the socket when he rose to his feet. Having gazed cautiously round him, and listened intently, he gently undid the fastenings of the door, and looked abroad.

It was a cold, dark night. The stars seemed, to the boy's eyes, farther from the earth than he had ever seen them before; there was no wind; and the sombre shadows thrown by the trees upon the ground, looked sepulchral and deathlike, from being so still. He softly reclosed the door, and having availed himself of the expiring light of the candle to tie up in a handkerchief the few articles of wearing apparel he had, sat himself down upon a bench, to wait for morning.

With the first ray of light that struggled through the crevices in the shutters, Oliver arose, and again unbarred the door. One timid look around – one moment's pause of hesitation – he had closed it behind him, and was in the open street.

He looked to the right and to the left, uncertain whither to fly. He remembered to have seen the waggons, as they went out, toiling up the hill. He took the same route; and arriving at a footpath across the fields: which he knew, after some distance, led out again into the road: struck into it, and walked quickly on.

CHAPTER 7

OLIVER WALKS TO LONDON. HE ENCOUNTERS ON THE ROAD A STRANGE SORT OF YOUNG GENTLEMAN

Oliver reached the stile at which the by-path terminated; and once more gained the high-road. It was eight o'clock now. Though he was nearly five miles away from the town, he ran, and hid behind the hedges, by turns, till noon: fearing that he might be pursued and overtaken. Then he sat down to rest by the side of the milestone, and began to think, for the first time, where he had better go and try to live.

Oliver walked twenty miles that day; and all that time tasted nothing but the crust of dry bread, and a few draughts of water, which he begged at the cottage-doors by the roadside. When the night came, he turned into a meadow; and, creeping close under a hay-rick, determined to lie there, till morning. He felt frightened at first, for the wind moaned dismally over the empty fields: and he was cold and hungry, and more alone than he had ever felt before. Being very tired with his walk, however, he soon fell asleep and forgot his troubles.

Early on the seventh morning after he had left his native place, Oliver limped slowly into the little town of Barnet.

By degrees, the shutters were opened; the window-blinds were drawn up; and people began passing to and fro. Some few stopped to gaze at

Oliver for a moment or two, or turned round to stare at him as they hurried by; but none relieved him, or troubled themselves to inquire how he came there. He had no heart to beg. And there he sat.

He had been crouching on the step for some time: wondering at the great number of public-houses when he was roused by observing that a boy, who had passed him carelessly some minutes before, had returned, and was now surveying him most earnestly from the opposite side of the way. He took little heed of this at first; but the boy remained in the same attitude of close observation so long, that Oliver raised his head, and returned his steady look. Upon this, the boy crossed over; and walking close up to Oliver, said,

"Hullo, my covey! What's the row?"

The boy who addressed this inquiry to the young wayfarer, was about his own age: but one of the queerest looking boys that Oliver had ever seen. He was a snub-nosed, flat-browed, common-faced boy enough; and as dirty a juvenile as one would wish to see; but he had about him all the airs and manners of a man. He was short of his age: with rather bow-legs, and little, sharp, ugly eyes. His hat was stuck on the top of his head so lightly, that it threatened to fall off every moment – and would have done so, very often, if the wearer had not had a knack of every now and then giving his head a sudden twitch, which brought it back to its old place again. He wore a man's coat, which reached nearly to his heels.

He had turned the cuffs back, halfway up his arm, to get his hands out of the sleeves: apparently with the ultimate view of thrusting them into the pockets of his corduroy trousers; for there he kept them. He was, altogether, as roystering and swaggering a young gentleman as ever stood four feet six, or something less, in his bluchers.

"Hullo, my covey! What's the row?" said this strange young gentleman to Oliver.

"I am very hungry and tired," replied Oliver: the tears standing in his eyes as he spoke. "I have walked a long way. I have been walking these seven days."

Assisting Oliver to rise, the young gentleman took him to an adjacent chandler's shop, where he purchased a sufficiency of ready-dressed ham and a half-quartern loaf, or, as he himself expressed it, "a fourpenny bran!" the ham being kept clean and preserved from dust, by the ingenious expedient of making a hole in the loaf by pulling out a portion of the crumb, and stuffing it therein. Taking the bread under his arm, the young gentleman turned into a small public-house, and led the way to a tap-room in the rear of the premises. Here, a pot of beer was brought in, by direction of the mysterious youth; and Oliver, falling to, at his new friend's bidding, made a long and hearty meal, during the progress of which, the strange boy eyed him from time to time with great attention.

"Going to London?" said the strange boy, when Oliver had at length concluded.

"Yes."

"Got any lodgings?"

"No."

"Money?"

"No."

The strange boy whistled; and put his arms into his pockets, as far as the big coat sleeves would let them go.

"Do you live in London?" inquired Oliver.

"Yes. I do, when I'm at home," replied the boy. "I suppose you want some place to sleep in tonight, don't you?"

"I do, indeed," answered Oliver. "I have not slept under a roof since I left the country."

"Don't fret your eyelids on that score," said the young gentleman. "I've got to be in London tonight; and I know a 'spectable old genelman as lives there, wot'll give you lodgings for nothink, and never ask for the change – that is, if any genelman he knows interduces you. And don't he know me? Oh, no! Not in the least! By no means. Certainly not!"

The young gentleman smiled, as if to intimate that the latter fragments of discourse were playfully ironical; and finished the beer as he did so.

This unexpected offer of shelter was too tempting to be resisted; especially as it was immediately followed up, by the assurance that the old gentleman referred to, would doubtless provide Oliver with a comfortable place, without loss of time. This led to a more friendly and confidential dialogue; from which Oliver discovered that his friend's name was Jack Dawkins, and that he was a peculiar pet and *protégé* of the elderly gentleman before mentioned. Among his intimate friends he was better known by the *sobriquet* of 'The artful Dodger'.

As John Dawkins objected to their entering London before nightfall, it was nearly eleven o'clock when they reached the turnpike at Islington.

There were a good many small shops; but the only stock in trade appeared to be heaps of children, who, even at that time of night, were crawling in and out at the doors, or screaming from the inside.

Oliver was just considering whether he hadn't better run away, when they reached the bottom of the hill. His conductor, catching him by the arm, pushed open the door of a house near Field Lane; and, drawing him into the passage, closed it behind them.

"Now, then!" cried a voice from below, in reply to a whistle from the Dodger.

Oliver, groping his way with one hand, and having the other firmly grasped by his companion, ascended with much difficulty the dark and broken stairs: which his conductor mounted with an ease and expedition that showed he was well acquainted with them. He threw open the door of a back-room, and drew Oliver in after him.

The walls and ceiling of the room were perfectly black with age and dirt. There was a deal table before the fire: upon which were a candle, stuck in a ginger-beer bottle, two or three pewter pots, a loaf and butter, and a plate. In a frying pan, which was on the fire, and which was secured to the mantelshelf by a string, some sausages were cooking; and standing over them, with a toasting-fork in his hand, was a very old shrivelled man, whose villainous-looking and repulsive face was obscured by a quantity of matted red hair. He was dressed in a greasy flannel gown, with his throat bare; and seemed to be dividing his attention between the frying pan and a clothes-horse, over which a great number of silk handkerchiefs were hanging. Several rough beds made of old sacks, were huddled side by side on the floor. Seated round the table were four or five boys, none older than the Dodger, smoking long clay pipes, and drinking spirits with the air of middle-aged men. These all crowded about their

associate as he whispered a few words to the old man; and then turned round and grinned at Oliver. So did the old man himself, toasting-fork in hand.

"This is him, Fagin," said Jack Dawkins; "my friend Oliver Twist."

The old man grinned; and, making a low obeisance to Oliver, took him by the hand, and hoped he should have the honour of his intimate acquaintance. Upon this, the young gentlemen with the pipes came round him, and shook both his hands very hard – especially the one in which he held his little bundle. One young gentleman was very anxious to hang up his cap for him; and another was so obliging as to put his hands in his pockets, in order that, as he was very tired, he might not have the trouble of emptying them, himself, when he went to bed. These civilities would probably have been extended much farther, but for a liberal exercise of the old man's toasting-fork on the heads and shoulders of the affectionate youths who offered them.

"We are very glad to see you, Oliver, very," said the old man. "Dodger, take off the sausages; and draw a tub near the fire for Oliver. Ah, you're a-staring at the pocket-handkerchiefs! eh, my dear. There are a good many of 'em, ain't there? We've just looked 'em out, ready for the wash; that's all, Oliver; that's all. Ha! ha! ha!"

The latter part of this speech, was hailed by a boisterous shout from all the hopeful pupils of the merry old gentleman. In the midst of which they went to supper.

Oliver ate his share, and Fagin then mixed him a glass of hot gin-and-water: telling him he must drink it off directly, because another gentleman wanted the tumbler. Oliver did as he was desired. Immediately afterwards he felt himself gently lifted on to one of the sacks; and then he sunk into a deep sleep.

CHAPTER 8

CONTAINING FURTHER PARTICULARS CONCERNING THE PLEASANT OLD GENTLEMAN AND HIS HOPEFUL PUPILS

It was late next morning when Oliver awoke, from a sound, long sleep. There was no other person in the room but Fagin, who was boiling some coffee in a saucepan for breakfast, and whistling softly to himself as he stirred it round and round, with an iron spoon. He would stop every now and then to listen when there was the least noise below: and when he had satisfied himself, he would go on, whistling and stirring again, as before.

Oliver saw the old man with his half-closed eyes; heard his low whistling; and recognized the sound of the spoon grating against the saucepan's sides; and yet the self-same senses were mentally engaged, at the same time, in busy action with almost everybody he had ever known.

When the coffee was done, the old man drew the saucepan to the hob. Standing, then, in an irresolute attitude for a few minutes, as if he did not well know how to employ himself, he turned round and looked at Oliver, and called him by his name. He did not answer, and was to all appearance asleep.

After satisfying himself upon this head, the old man stepped gently to the door: which he fastened. He then drew forth: as it seemed to Oliver, from some trap in the floor: a small box, which he placed carefully on the table. His eyes glistened as he raised the lid, and looked in. Dragging an old chair to the table, he sat down; and took from it a magnificent gold watch, sparkling with jewels.

"Ah!" said the old man, shrugging up his shoulders, and distorting every feature with a hideous grin. "Clever dogs! Clever dogs! Staunch to the last! Never told the old parson where they were. Never peached upon old Fagin! And why should they? It wouldn't have loosened the knot, or kept the drop up, a minute longer. No, no, no! Fine fellows! Fine fellows!"

As the old man uttered these words, his bright dark eyes, which had been staring vacantly before him, fell on Oliver's face; the boy's eyes were fixed on his in mute curiosity; and although the recognition was only for

an instant – for the briefest space of time that can possibly be conceived – it was enough to show the old man that he had been observed.

He closed the lid of the box with a loud crash; and, laying his hand on a bread knife which was on the table, started furiously up. He trembled very much though; for, even in his terror Oliver could see that the knife quivered in the air.

"What's that?" said the old man. "What do you watch me for? Why are you awake? What have you seen? Speak out, boy! Quick – quick! for your life."

"I wasn't able to sleep any longer, sir," replied Oliver, meekly. "I am very sorry if I disturbed you, sir."

"You were not awake an hour ago?" said the old man, scowling fiercely on the boy.

"No! No, indeed!" replied Oliver.

"Are you sure?" cried the old man: with a still fiercer look than before: and a threatening attitude.

"Upon my word I was not, sir," replied Oliver, earnestly. "I was not, indeed, sir."

"Tush, tush, my dear!" said the old man, abruptly resuming his old manner, and playing with the knife a little, before he laid it down; as if to induce the belief that he had caught it up, in mere sport. "Of course I know that, my dear. I only tried to frighten you. You're a brave boy. Ha! ha! you're a brave boy, Oliver!" The old man rubbed his hands with a chuckle, but glanced uneasily at the box, notwithstanding.

"Did you see any of these pretty things, my dear?" said the old man, laying his hand upon it after a short pause.

"Yes, sir," replied Oliver.

"Ah!" said the old man, turning rather pale. "They – they're mine,

Oliver; my little property. All I have to live upon, in my old age. The folks call me a miser, my dear. Only a miser; that's all."

Oliver thought the old gentleman must be a decided miser to live in such a dirty place, with so many watches; but, thinking that perhaps his fondness for the Dodger and the other boys, cost him a good deal of money, he only cast a deferential look at Fagin, and asked if he might get up.

"Certainly, my dear, certainly," replied the old gentleman. "Stay. There's a pitcher of water in the corner by the door. Bring it here; and I'll give you a basin to wash in, my dear."

Oliver got up; walked across the room; and stooped for an instant to raise the pitcher. When he turned his head, the box was gone.

He had scarcely washed himself, and made everything tidy, by emptying the basin out of the window, agreeably to the old man's directions, when the Dodger returned: accompanied by a very sprightly young friend, whom Oliver had seen smoking on the previous night, and who was now formally introduced to him as Charley Bates. The four sat down, to breakfast on the coffee, and some hot rolls and ham, which the Dodger had brought home in the crown of his hat.

"Well," said the old man, glancing slyly at Oliver, and addressing himself to the Dodger, "I hope you've been at work this morning, my dears?"

"Hard," replied the Dodger.

"As nails," added Charley Bates.

"Good boys, good boys!" said the old man. "What have *you* got, Dodger?"

"A couple of pocket-books," replied that young gentleman.

"Lined?" inquired the old man, with eagerness.

"Pretty well," replied the Dodger, producing two pocket-books; one green, and the other red.

"Not so heavy as they might be," said the old man, after looking at the insides carefully; "but very neat and nicely made. Ingenious workman, ain't he, Oliver?"

"Very, indeed, sir," said Oliver. At which Mr Charles Bates laughed uproariously; very much to the amazement of Oliver, who saw nothing to laugh at, in anything that had passed.

"And what have you got, my dear?" said Fagin to Charley Bates.

"Wipes," replied Master Bates; at the same time producing four pocket-handkerchiefs.

"Well," said the old man, inspecting them closely; "they're very good ones, very. You haven't marked them well, though, Charley; so the marks shall be picked out with a needle, and we'll teach Oliver how to do it. Shall us, Oliver, eh? Ha! ha! ha!"

"If you please, sir," said Oliver.

"You'd like to be able to make pocket-handkerchiefs as easy as Charley Bates, wouldn't you, my dear?" said the old man.

"Very much, indeed, if you'll teach me, sir," replied Oliver.

Master Bates saw something so exquisitely ludicrous in this reply that he burst into another laugh; which laugh, meeting the coffee he was drinking, and carrying it down some wrong channel, very nearly terminated in his premature suffocation.

"He is so jolly green!" said Charley when he recovered, as an apology to the company for his unpolite behaviour.

The Dodger said nothing, but he smoothed Oliver's hair over his eyes, and said he'd know better, by-and-bye; upon which the old gentleman, observing Oliver's colour mounting, changed the subject by asking whether there had been much of a crowd at the execution that morning? This made him wonder more and more; for it was plain from the replies of the two boys that they had both been there; and Oliver naturally wondered how they could possibly have found time to be so very industrious.

When the breakfast was cleared away, the merry old gentleman and the two boys played at a very curious and uncommon game, which was performed in this way. The merry old gentleman, placing a snuff-box in one pocket of his trousers, a note-case in the other, and a watch in his waistcoat pocket, with a guard-chain round his neck, and sticking a mock diamond pin in his shirt: buttoned his coat tight round him, and putting his spectacle-case and handkerchief in his pockets, trotted up and down the room with a stick, in imitation of the manner in which old gentlemen walk about the streets any hour in the day. Sometimes he stopped at the fire-place, and sometimes at the door, making believe that he was staring with all his might into shop-windows. At such times he would look constantly round him, for fear of thieves, and would keep slapping all his pockets in turn, to see that he hadn't lost anything, in such a very funny and natural manner, that Oliver laughed till the tears ran down his face. All this time, the two boys followed him closely about: getting out of his sight, so nimbly, every time he turned round, that it was impossible to follow their motions. At last, the Dodger trod upon his toes, or ran upon his boot accidentally, while Charley Bates stumbled up against him behind; and in that one moment they took from him, with the most extraordinary rapidity, snuff-box, note-case, watch-guard, chain, shirt-pin, pocket-handkerchief, even the spectacle-case. If the old gentleman felt a hand in any one of his pockets, he cried out where it was; and then the game began all over again.

When this game had been played a great many times, a couple of young ladies called to see the young gentlemen; one of whom was named Bet, and the other Nancy. They wore a good deal of hair, not very neatly

turned up behind, and were rather untidy about the shoes and stockings. They were not exactly pretty, perhaps; but they had a great deal of colour in their faces, and looked quite stout and hearty. Being remarkably free and agreeable in their manners, Oliver thought them very nice girls indeed. As there is no doubt they were.

These visitors stopped a long time. Spirits were produced, in consequence of one of the young ladies complaining of a coldness in her inside; and the conversation took a very convivial and improving turn. At length, Charley Bates expressed his opinion that it was time to pad the hoof. This, it occurred to Oliver, must be French for going out; for, directly afterwards, the Dodger, and Charley, and the two young ladies, went away together, having been kindly furnished by the amiable old man with money to spend.

"There, my dear," said Fagin. "That's a pleasant life, isn't it? They have gone out for the day."

"Have they done work, sir?" inquired Oliver.

"Yes," said the old man: "that is, unless they should unexpectedly come across any, when they are out; and they won't neglect it, if they do, my dear, depend upon it. Make 'em your models, my dear. Make 'em your models," tapping the fire-shovel on the hearth to add force to his words; "do everything they bid you, and take their advice in all matters – especially the Dodger's, my dear. He'll be a great man himself, and will make you one too, if you take pattern by him. – Is my handkerchief hanging out of my pocket, my dear?" said the old man, stopping short.

"Yes, sir," said Oliver.

"See if you can take it out, without my feeling it: as you saw them do, when we were at play this morning."

Oliver held up the bottom of the pocket with one hand, as he had seen the Dodger hold it, and drew the handkerchief lightly out of it with the other.

"Is it gone?" cried the old man.

"Here it is, sir," said Oliver, showing it in his hand.

"You're a clever boy, my dear," said the playful old gentleman, patting Oliver on the head approvingly. "I never saw a sharper lad. Here's a shilling for you. If you go on, in this way, you'll be the greatest man of the time. And now come here, and I'll show you how to take the marks out of the handkerchiefs."

Oliver wondered what picking the old gentleman's pocket in play, had to do with his chances of being a great man. But, thinking that the old man, being so much his senior, must know best, he followed him quietly to the table, and was soon deeply involved in his new study.

CHAPTER 9

OLIVER BECOMES BETTER ACQUAINTED WITH THE CHARACTERS OF HIS NEW ASSOCIATES; AND PURCHASES EXPERIENCE AT A HIGH PRICE. BEING A SHORT, BUT VERY IMPORTANT CHAPTER, IN THIS HISTORY

For many days, Oliver remained in the old man's room, picking the marks out of the pocket-handkerchiefs (of which a great number were brought home), and sometimes taking part in the game already described: which the two boys and the old man played, regularly, every morning. At length, he began to languish for fresh air, and took many occasions of earnestly entreating the old gentleman to allow him to go out to work, with his two companions.

At length, one morning, Oliver obtained the permission he had so eagerly sought. There had been no handkerchiefs to work upon, for two or three days, and the dinners had been rather meagre. Perhaps these were reasons for the old gentleman's giving his assent; but, whether they were or no, he told Oliver he might go, and placed him under the joint guardianship of Charley Bates, and his friend the Dodger.

The three boys sallied out; the Dodger with his coat-sleeves tucked up, and his hat cocked, as usual; Master Bates sauntering along with his hands in his pockets; and Oliver between them, wondering where they were going, and what branch of manufacture he would be instructed in, first.

They were just emerging from a narrow court not far from the open square in Clerkenwell, when the Dodger made a sudden stop; and, laying his finger on his lip, drew his companions back again, with the greatest caution and circumspection.

"What's the matter?" demanded Oliver.

"Hush!" replied the Dodger. "Do you see that old cove at the book-stall?"

"The old gentleman over the way?" said Oliver. "Yes, I see him."

"He'll do," said the Dodger.

"A prime plant," observed Master Charley Bates.

Oliver looked from one to the other, with the greatest surprise; but he was not permitted to make any inquiries; for the two boys walked stealthily across the road, and slunk close behind the old gentleman towards whom his attention had been directed. Oliver walked a few paces after them; and, not knowing whether to advance or retire, stood looking on in silent amazement.

The old gentleman was a very respectable-looking personage, with a powdered head and gold spectacles. He had taken up a book from the stall, and there he stood, reading away. It was plain, from his abstraction, that he saw not the book-stall, nor the street, nor the boys, nor, in short, anything but the book itself.

What was Oliver's horror and alarm as he stood a

few paces off, looking on with his eyelids as wide open as they would possibly go, to see the Dodger plunge his hand into the old gentleman's pocket, and draw from thence a handkerchief! To see him hand the same to Charley Bates; and finally to behold them, both, running away round the corner at full speed!

In an instant the whole mystery of the hankerchiefs, and the watches, and the jewels, and Fagin, rushed upon the boy's mind. He stood, for a moment, with the blood so tingling through all his veins from terror, that he felt as if he were in a burning fire; then, confused and frightened, he took to his heels; and, not knowing what he did, made off as fast as he could lay his feet to the ground.

This was all done in a minute's space. In the very instant when Oliver began to run, the old gentleman, putting his hand to his pocket, and missing his handkerchief, turned sharp round. Seeing the boy scudding

BOOKS
OLD BELL TA

away at such a rapid pace, he very naturally concluded him to be the depredator; and, shouting "Stop thief!" with all his might, made off after him, book in hand.

But the old gentleman was not the only person who raised the hue-and-cry. The Dodger and Master Bates, unwilling to attract public attention by running down the open street, had merely retired into the very first doorway round the corner. They no sooner heard the cry, and saw Oliver running, than, guessing exactly how the matter stood, they issued forth with great promptitude; and, shouting "Stop thief!" too, joined in the pursuit like good citizens.

"Stop thief! Stop thief!" There is a magic in the sound. The tradesman leaves his counter, and the carman his waggon; the butcher throws down his tray; the baker his basket; the milkman his pail; the errand-boy his parcels; the school-boy his marbles; the paviour his pick-axe; the child his battledore. Away they run, pell-mell, helter-skelter, slap-dash: tearing, yelling, screaming, knocking down the passengers as they turn the corners, rousing up the dogs, and astonishing the fowls: and streets, squares, and courts, re-echo with the sound.

"Stop thief! Stop thief!" There is a passion *for hunting something* deeply implanted in the human breast. One wretched breathless child, panting with exhaustion; terror in his looks; agony in his eyes; large drops of perspiration streaming down his face; strains every nerve to make head upon his pursuers; and as they follow on his track, and gain upon him every instant, they hail his decreasing strength with joy. "Stop thief!" Ay, stop him for God's sake, were it only in mercy!

Stopped at last! A clever blow. He is down upon the pavement; and the crowd eagerly gather round him: each new comer, jostling and struggling with the others to catch a glimpse. "Stand aside!" "Give him a little air!"

"Nonsense! he don't deserve it." "Where's the gentleman?" "Here he is, coming down the street." "Make room there for the gentleman!" "Is this the boy, sir!" "Yes."

Oliver lay, covered with mud and dust, and bleeding from the mouth, looking wildly round upon the heap of faces that surrounded him, when the old gentleman was officiously dragged and pushed into the circle by the foremost of the pursuers.

"Yes," said the gentleman, "I am afraid it is the boy."

"Afraid!" murmured the crowd. "That's a good 'un!"

"Poor fellow!" said the gentleman, "he has hurt himself."

"*I* did that, sir," said a great lubberly fellow, stepping forward; "and preciously I cut my knuckle agin' his mouth. *I* stopped him, sir."

The fellow touched his hat with a grin, expecting something for his pains; but, the old gentleman, eyeing him with an expression of dislike, looked anxiously round, as if he contemplated running away himself: which it is very possible he might have attempted to do, and thus have afforded another chase, had not a police officer (who is generally the last person to arrive in such cases) at that moment made his way through the crowd, and seized Oliver by the collar. "Come, get up," said the man, roughly.

"It wasn't me indeed, sir. Indeed, indeed, it was two other boys," said Oliver, clasping his hands passionately, and looking round. "They are here somewhere."

"Oh no, they ain't," said the officer. He meant this to be ironical, but it was true besides; for the Dodger and Charley Bates had filed off down the first convenient court they came to. "Come, get up!"

"Don't hurt him," said the old gentleman, compassionately.

"Oh no, I won't hurt him," replied the officer, tearing his jacket half off his back, in proof thereof. "Come, I know you; it won't do. Will you stand upon your legs, you young devil?"

Oliver, who could hardly stand, made a shift to raise himself on his feet, and was at once lugged along the streets by the jacket-collar, at a rapid pace. The gentleman walked on with them by the officer's side; and as many of the crowd as could achieve the feat, got a little ahead, and stared back at Oliver from time to time. The boys shouted in triumph; and on they went.

CHAPTER 10

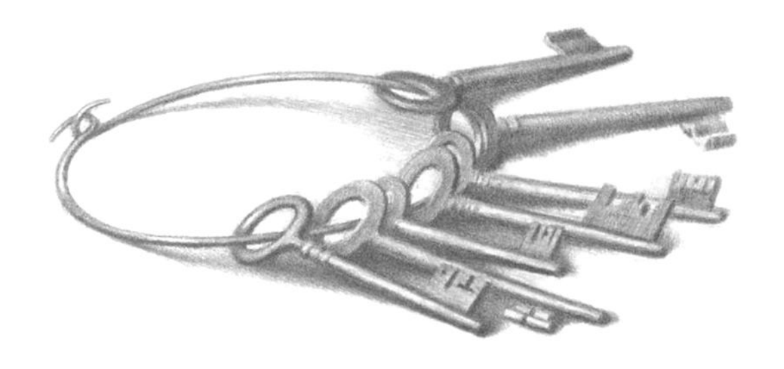

TREATS OF MR FANG THE POLICE MAGISTRATE; AND FURNISHES A SLIGHT SPECIMEN OF HIS MODE OF ADMINISTERING JUSTICE

The offence had been committed within the district, and indeed in the immediate neighbourhood of, a very notorious metropolitan police office. The crowd had only the satisfaction of accompanying Oliver through two or three streets, and down a place called Mutton Hill, when he was led beneath a low archway, and up a dirty court, into this dispensary of summary justice, by the back way. It was a small paved yard into which they turned; and here they encountered a stout man with a bunch of whiskers on his face, and a bunch of keys in his hand.

"What's the matter now?" said the man carelessly.

"A young fogle-hunter," replied the man who had Oliver in charge.

"Are you the party that's been robbed, sir?" inquired the man with the keys.

"Yes, I am," replied the old gentleman; "but I am not sure that this boy actually took the handkerchief. I – I would rather not press the case."

"Must go before the magistrate now, sir," replied the man. "His worship will be disengaged in half a minute. Now, young gallows!"

This was an invitation for Oliver to enter through a door which he unlocked as he spoke, and which led into a stone cell. Here he was searched; and nothing being found upon him, locked up.

This cell was in shape and size something like an area cellar, only not so light. It was most intolerably dirty; for it was Monday morning; and it had been tenanted by six drunken people, who had been locked up, elsewhere, since Saturday night. But this is little. In our station-houses, men and women are every night confined on the most trivial *charges* – the word is worth noting – in dungeons, compared with which, those in Newgate, occupied by the most atrocious felons, tried, found guilty, and under sentence of death, are palaces. Let any one who doubts this, compare the two.

The old gentleman looked almost as rueful as Oliver when the key grated in the lock. He turned with a sigh to the book, which had been the innocent cause of all this disturbance.

"There is something in that boy's face," said the old gentleman to himself as he walked slowly away, tapping his chin with the cover of the book, in a thoughtful manner; "something that touches and interests me. *Can* he be innocent? He looked like. – By the bye," exclaimed the old gentleman, halting very abruptly, and staring up into the sky, "Bless my soul! Where have I seen something like that look before?"

After musing for some minutes, the old gentleman walked, with the same meditative face, into a back ante-room opening from the yard; and there, retiring into a corner, called up before his mind's eye a vast amphitheatre of faces over which a dusky curtain had hung for many years. "No," said the old gentleman, shaking his head; "it must be imagination." The old gentleman could recall no one countenance of which Oliver's features bore a trace. So, he heaved a sigh over the recollections he had awakened; and being, happily for himself, an absent old gentleman, buried them again in the pages of the musty book.

He was roused by a touch on the shoulder, and a request from the man with the keys to follow him into the office. He closed his book hastily; and was at once ushered into the imposing presence of the renowned Mr Fang.

The office was a front parlour, with a panelled wall. Mr Fang sat behind a bar, at the upper end; and on one side the door was a sort of wooden pen in which poor little Oliver was already deposited: trembling very much at the awfulness of the scene.

Mr Fang was a lean, long-backed, stiff-necked, middle-sized man, with no great quantity of hair, and what he had, growing on the back and sides of his head. His face was stern, and much flushed. If he were really not in the habit of drinking rather more than was exactly good for him, he might have brought an action against his countenance for libel, and have recovered heavy damages.

The old gentleman bowed respectfully; and advancing to the magistrate's desk, said, suiting the action to the word, "That is my name and address, sir." He then withdrew a pace or two; and, with another polite and gentlemanly inclination of the head, waited to be questioned.

"Who are you?" said Mr Fang.

The old gentleman pointed, with some surprise, to his card.

"Officer!" said Mr Fang, tossing the card contemptuously away with the newspaper. "Who is this fellow?"

"My name, sir," said the old gentleman, speaking *like* a gentleman, "my name, sir, is Brownlow. Permit me to inquire the name of the magistrate who offers a gratuitous and unprovoked insult to a respectable person, under the protection of the bench." Saying this, Mr Brownlow looked round the office as if in search of some person who would afford him the required information.

"Officer!" said Mr Fang, throwing the paper on one side, "what's this fellow charged with?"

"He's not charged at all, your worship," replied the officer. "He appears against the boy, your worship."

His worship knew this perfectly well; but it was a good annoyance, and a safe one.

"Appears against the boy, does he?" said Fang, surveying Mr Brownlow contemptuously from head to foot. "Swear him!"

"Before I am sworn, I must beg to say one word," said Mr Brownlow: "and that is, that I really never, without actual experience, could have believed—"

"Hold your tongue, sir!" said Mr Fang, peremptorily.

"I will not, sir!" replied the old gentleman.

"Hold your tongue this instant, or I'll have you turned out of the office!" said Mr Fang. "You're an insolent, impertinent fellow. How dare you bully a magistrate!"

"What!" exclaimed the old gentleman, reddening.

"Swear this person!" said Fang to the clerk. "I'll not hear another word. Swear him."

Mr Brownlow's indignation was greatly roused; but reflecting perhaps, that he might only injure the boy by giving vent to it, he suppressed his feelings and submitted to be sworn at once.

"Now," said Fang, "what's the charge against this boy? What have you got to say, sir?"

"I was standing at a book-stall—" Mr Brownlow began.

"Hold your tongue, sir," said Mr Fang. "Policeman! Where's the policeman? Here, swear this policeman. Now, policeman, what is this?"

The policeman, with becoming humility, related how he had taken the charge; how he had searched Oliver, and found nothing on his person; and how that was all he knew about it.

"Are there any witnesses?" inquired Mr Fang.

"None, your worship," replied the policeman.

Mr Fang sat silent for some minutes, and then, turning round to the prosecutor, said in a towering passion,

"Do you mean to state what your complaint against this boy is, man, or do you not? You have been sworn. Now, if you stand there, refusing to give evidence, I'll punish you for disrespect to the bench; I will, by—"

By what, or by whom, nobody knows, for the clerk and jailer coughed very loud, just at the right moment; and the former dropped a heavy book upon the floor, thus preventing the words from being heard – accidentally, of course.

With many interruptions, and repeated insults, Mr Brownlow contrived to state his case; observing that, in the surprise of the moment, he had run after the boy because he saw him running away; and expressing his hope that, if the magistrate should believe him, although not actually the thief, to be connected with the thieves, he would deal as leniently with him as justice would allow.

"He has been hurt already," said the old gentleman in conclusion. "And I fear," he added, with great energy, looking towards the bar, "I really fear that he is ill."

"Oh! yes, I dare say!" said Mr Fang, with a sneer. "Come, none of your tricks here, you young vagabond; they won't do. What's your name?"

Oliver tried to reply, but his tongue failed him. He was deadly pale; and the whole place seemed turning round and round.

"What's your name, you hardened scoundrel?" demanded Mr Fang. "Officer, what's his name?"

This was addressed to a bluff old fellow, in a striped waistcoat, who was standing by the bar. He bent over Oliver, and repeated the inquiry; but finding him really incapable of understanding the question; and knowing that his not replying would only infuriate the magistrate the more, and add to the severity of his sentence; he hazarded a guess.

"He says his name's Tom White, your worship," said the kind-hearted thief-taker.

"Oh, he won't speak out, won't he?" said Fang. "Very well, very well. Where does he live?"

"Where he can, your worship," replied the officer; again pretending to receive Oliver's answer.

"Has he any parents?" inquired Mr Fang.

"He says they died in his infancy, your worship," replied the officer: hazarding the usual reply.

At this point of the inquiry, Oliver raised his head; and, looking round with imploring eyes, murmured a feeble prayer for a draught of water.

"Stuff and nonsense!" said Mr Fang: "don't try to make a fool of me."

"I think he really is ill, your worship," remonstrated the officer.

"I know better," said Mr Fang.

"Take care of him, officer," said the old gentleman, raising his hands instinctively; "he'll fall down."

"Stand away, officer," cried Fang; "let him, if he likes."

Oliver availed himself of the kind permission, and fell to the floor in a fainting fit. The men in the office looked at each other, but no one dared to stir.

"I knew he was shamming," said Fang, as if this were incontestable proof of the fact. "Let him lie there; he'll soon be tired of that."

"How do you propose to deal with the case, sir?" inquired the clerk in a low voice.

"Summarily," replied Mr Fang. "He stands committed for three months – hard labour of course. Clear the office."

The door was opened for this purpose, and a couple of men were preparing to carry the insensible boy to his cell; when an elderly man of decent but poor appearance, clad in an old suit of black, rushed hastily into the office, and advanced towards the bench.

"Stop, stop! Don't take him away! For Heaven's sake stop a moment!" cried the new-comer, breathless with haste.

Although the presiding Genii in such an office as this, exercise a summary and arbitrary power over the liberties, the good name, the character, almost the lives, of Her Majesty's subjects, especially of the poorer class; and although, within such walls, enough fantastic tricks are daily played to make the angels blind with weeping; they are closed to the public, save through the medium of the daily press. Mr Fang was consequently not a little indignant to see an unbidden guest enter in such irreverent disorder.

"What is this? Who is this? Turn this man out. Clear the office!" cried Mr Fang.

"I *will* speak," cried the man; "I will not be turned out. I saw it all. I keep the book-stall. I demand to be sworn. I will not be put down. Mr Fang, you must hear me. You must not refuse, sir."

The man was right. His manner was determined; and the matter was growing rather too serious to be hushed up.

"Swear the man," growled Mr Fang, with a very ill grace. "Now, man, what have you got to say?"

"This," said the man: "I saw three boys: two others and the prisoner here: loitering on the opposite side of the way, when this gentleman was reading. The robbery was committed by another boy. I saw it done; and I saw that this boy was perfectly amazed and stupefied by it." Having by this time recovered a little breath, the worthy book-stall keeper proceeded to relate, in a more coherent manner, the exact circumstances of the robbery.

"Why didn't you come here before?" said Fang, after a pause.

"I hadn't a soul to mind the shop," replied the man. "Everybody who could have helped me, had joined in the pursuit. I could get nobody till five minutes ago; and I've run here all the way."

"The prosecutor was reading, was he?" inquired Fang, after another pause.

"Yes," replied the man. "The very book he has in his hand."

"Oh, that book, eh?" said Fang. "Is it paid for?"

"No, it is not," replied the man, with a smile.

"Dear me, I forgot all about it!" exclaimed the absent old gentleman, innocently.

"A nice person to prefer a charge against a poor boy!" said Fang, with a comical effort to look humane. "I consider, sir, that you have

obtained possession of that book, under very suspicious and disreputable circumstances; and you may think yourself very fortunate that the owner of the property declines to prosecute. Let this be a lesson to you, my man, or the law will overtake you yet. The boy is discharged. Clear the office."

"D—n me!" cried the old gentleman, bursting out with the rage he had kept down so long, "d— me! I'll—"

"Clear the office!" said the magistrate. "Officers, do you hear? Clear the office!"

The mandate was obeyed; and the indignant Mr Brownlow was conveyed out, with the book in one hand, and the bamboo cane in the other: in a perfect frenzy of rage and defiance. He reached the yard; and his passion vanished in a moment. Little Oliver Twist lay on his back on the pavement, with his shirt unbuttoned, and his temples bathed with water; his face a deadly white; and a cold tremble convulsing his whole frame.

"Poor boy, poor boy!" said Mr Brownlow, bending over him. "Call a coach, somebody, pray. Directly!"

A coach was obtained, and Oliver having been carefully laid on one seat, the old gentleman got in and sat himself on the other.

"May I accompany you?" said the book-stall keeper, looking in.

"Bless me, yes, my dear sir," said Mr Brownlow quickly. "I forgot you. Dear, dear! I have this unhappy book still! Jump in. Poor fellow! There's no time to lose."

The book-stall keeper got into the coach; and away they drove.

CHAPTER 11

IN WHICH OLIVER IS TAKEN BETTER CARE OF THAN HE EVER WAS BEFORE

The coach rattled away, over nearly the same ground as that which Oliver had traversed when he first entered London in company with the Dodger; and, turning a different way when it reached the Angel at Islington, stopped at length before a neat house, in a quiet shady street near Pentonville. Here, a bed was prepared, without loss of time, in which Mr Brownlow saw his young charge carefully and comfortably deposited; and here, he was tended with a kindness and solicitude that knew no bounds.

But, for many days, Oliver remained insensible to all the goodness of his new friends. The sun rose and sank, and rose and sank again, and many times after that; and still the boy lay stretched on his uneasy bed, dwindling away beneath the dry and wasting heat of fever. The worm does not his work more surely on the dead body, than does this slow creeping fire upon the living frame.

Weak, and thin, and pallid, he awoke at last from what seemed to have been a long and troubled dream. The crisis of the disease was safely past. He belonged to the world again.

In three days' time he was able to sit in an easy-chair, well propped up with pillows; and, as he was still too weak to walk, Mrs Bedwin, the housekeeper, had him carried downstairs into the little housekeeper's room, which belonged to her. Having sat him, here, by the fireside, the good old lady sat herself down too; and, being in a state of considerable delight at seeing him so much better, forthwith began to cry most violently.

"Never mind me, my dear," said the old lady. "I'm only having a regular good cry. There; it's all over now; and I'm quite comfortable."

"You're very, very kind to me, ma'am," said Oliver.

"Well, never you mind that, my dear," said the old lady; "that's got nothing to do with your broth; and it's full time you had it; for the doctor says Mr Brownlow may come in to see you this morning; and we must get up our best looks, because the better we look, the more he'll be pleased." And with this, the old lady applied herself to warming up, in a little saucepan, a basin full of broth: strong enough, Oliver thought, to furnish an ample dinner, when reduced to the regulation strength, for three hundred and fifty paupers, at the lowest computation.

"Are you fond of pictures, dear?" inquired the old lady, seeing that Oliver had fixed his eyes, most intently, on a portrait which hung against the wall; just opposite his chair.

"I don't quite know, ma'am," said Oliver, without taking his eyes from the canvas; "I have seen so few, that I hardly know. What a beautiful, mild face that lady's is!"

"Ah!" said the old lady, "painters always make ladies out prettier than they are, or they wouldn't get any custom, child. The man that invented the machine for taking likenesses might have known *that* would never succeed; it's a deal too honest. A deal," said the old lady, laughing very heartily at her own acuteness.

"Is – is that a likeness, ma'am?" said Oliver.

"Yes," said the old lady, looking up for a moment from the broth; "that's a portrait."

"Whose, ma'am?" asked Oliver.

"Why, really, my dear, I don't know," answered the old lady in a good-humoured manner. "It's not a likeness of anybody that you or I know, I expect. It seems to strike your fancy, dear."

"It is so very pretty," replied Oliver.

"Why, sure you're not afraid of it?" said the old lady: observing, in great surprise, the look of awe with which the child regarded the painting.

"Oh no, no," returned Oliver quickly; "but the eyes look so sorrowful; and where I sit, they seem fixed upon me. It makes my heart beat," added Oliver in a low voice, "as if it was alive, and wanted to speak to me, but couldn't."

"Lord save us!" exclaimed the old lady, starting; "don't talk in that way, child. You're weak and nervous after your illness. Let me wheel your chair round to the other side; and then you won't see it. There!" said the old lady, suiting the action to the word; "you don't see it now, at all events."

Oliver *did* see it in his mind's eye as distinctly as if he had not altered his position; but he thought it better not to worry the kind old lady; so he smiled gently when she looked at him; and Mrs Bedwin, satisfied that he felt more comfortable, salted and broke bits of toasted bread into the broth, with all the bustle befitting so solemn a preparation. Oliver got through it with extraordinary expedition. He had scarcely swallowed the last spoonful, when there came a soft rap at the door. "Come in," said the old lady; and in walked Mr Brownlow.

Now, the old gentleman came in as brisk as need be; but, he had no sooner raised his spectacles on his forehead, and thrust his hands behind the skirts of his dressing-gown to take a good look at Oliver, than his countenance underwent a very great variety of odd contortions. Oliver looked very worn and shadowy from sickness, and made an ineffectual attempt to stand up, out of respect to his benefactor, which terminated in his sinking back into the chair again; and the fact is, if the truth must be told, that Mr Brownlow's heart, being large enough for any six ordinary old gentlemen of humane disposition, forced a supply of tears into his eyes, by some hydraulic process which we are not sufficiently philosophical to be in a condition to explain.

"He has just had a basin of beautiful strong broth, sir," replied Mrs Bedwin: drawing herself up slightly.

"Ugh!" said Mr Brownlow, with a slight shudder; "a couple of glasses of port wine would have done him a great deal more good. Wouldn't they, Tom White, eh?"

"My name is Oliver, sir," replied the little invalid: with a look of great astonishment.

"Oliver," said Mr Brownlow; "Oliver what? Oliver White, eh?"

"No, sir, Twist, Oliver Twist."

"Queer name!" said the old gentleman. "What made you tell the magistrate your name was White?"

"I never told him so, sir," returned Oliver in amazement.

This sounded so like a falsehood, that the old gentleman looked somewhat sternly in Oliver's face. It was impossible to doubt him; there was truth in every one of its thin and sharpened lineaments.

"Some mistake," said Mr Brownlow. But, although his motive for looking steadily at Oliver no longer existed, the old idea of the resemblance between his features and some familiar face came upon him so strongly, that he could not withdraw his gaze.

"I hope you are not angry with me, sir?" said Oliver, raising his eyes beseechingly.

"No, no," replied the old gentleman. "Why! what's this? Bedwin, look there!"

As he spoke, he pointed hastily to the picture above Oliver's head, and then to the boy's face. There was its living copy. The eyes, the head, the mouth; every feature was the same. The expression was, for the instant, so precisely alike, that the minutest line seemed copied with startling accuracy!

Oliver knew not the cause of this sudden exclamation; for, not being strong enough to bear the start it gave him, he fainted away.

CHAPTER 12

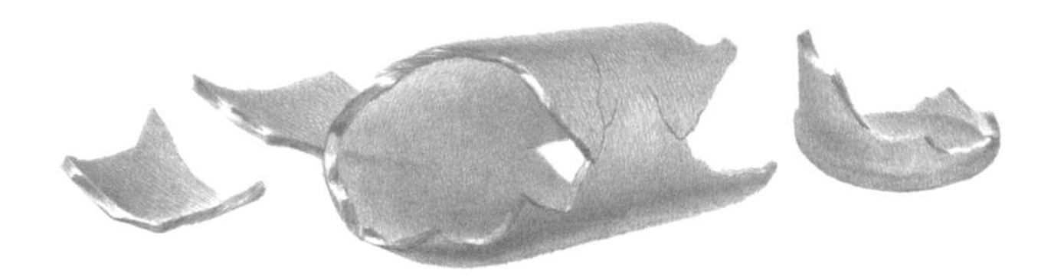

SOME NEW ACQUAINTANCES ARE INTRODUCED TO THE INTELLIGENT READER; CONNECTED WITH WHOM VARIOUS PLEASANT MATTERS ARE RELATED, APPERTAINING TO THIS HISTORY

"Where's Oliver?" said Fagin, rising with a menacing look. "Where's the boy?"

The young thieves eyed their preceptor as if they were alarmed at his violence; and looked uneasily at each other. But they made no reply.

"What's become of the boy?" said the old man, seizing the Dodger tightly by the collar, and threatening him with horrid imprecations. "Speak out, or I'll throttle you!"

"Why, the traps have got him, and that's all about it," said the Dodger, sullenly. "Come, let go o' me, will you!" And, swinging himself, at one jerk, clean out of the big coat, which he left in Fagin's hands, the Dodger snatched up the toasting fork, and made a pass at the merry old gentleman's waistcoat.

Fagin stepped back in this emergency, and, seizing up the pot, prepared to hurl it at his assailant's head. But Charley Bates, at this moment, calling his attention by a terrific howl, he suddenly altered its destination, and flung it full at that young gentleman.

"Why, what the blazes is in the wind now!" growled a deep voice.

Wot's it all about, Fagin? Come in, you sneaking warmint; wot are you stopping outside for, as if you was ashamed of your master! Come in!"

The man who growled out these words, was a stoutly-built fellow of about five-and-thirty, in a black velveteen coat, very soiled drab breeches, lace-up half boots, and grey cotton stockings, which inclosed a bulky pair of legs, with large swelling calves – the kind of legs, which in such costume, always look in an unfinished and incomplete state without a set of fetters to garnish them.

"Come in, d'ye hear?" growled this engaging ruffian.

A white shaggy dog, with his face scratched and torn in twenty different places, skulked into the room.

"Why didn't you come in afore?" said the man. "You're getting too proud to own me afore company, are you? Lie down!"

This command was accompanied with a kick, which sent the animal to the other end of the room. He appeared well used to it, however; for he coiled himself up in a corner very quietly, without uttering a sound, and winking his very ill-looking eyes twenty times in a minute, appeared to occupy himself in taking a survey of the apartment.

"Hush! hush! Mr Sikes," said the old man, trembling; "don't speak so loud!"

"None of your mistering," replied the ruffian; "you always mean mischief when you come that. You know my name: out with it! I shan't disgrace it when the time comes."

"Well, well, then – Bill Sikes," said the old man, with abject humility. "You seem out of humour, Bill."

"Perhaps I am," replied Sikes; "I should think *you* was rather out of sorts too, unless you mean as little harm when you throw pewter pots about."

After swallowing two or three glasses of spirits, Mr Sikes condescended to take some notice of the young gentlemen; which gracious act led to a conversation, in which the cause and manner of Oliver's capture were circumstantially detailed, with such alterations and improvements on the truth, as to the Dodger appeared most advisable under the circumstances.

"I'm afraid," said the old man, "that he may say something which will get us into trouble."

"That's very likely," returned Sikes with a malicious grin. "You're blowed upon, Fagin."

"And I'm afraid, you see," added the old man, speaking as if he had not noticed the interruption; and regarding the other closely as he did so – "I'm afraid that, if the game was up with us, it might be up with a good many more, and that it would come out rather worse for you than it would for me, my dear."

The man started, and turned round upon Fagin. But the old gentleman's shoulders were shrugged up to his ears; and his eyes were vacantly staring on the opposite wall.

"Somebody must find out wot's been done at the office," said Mr Sikes.

Fagin nodded assent.

The prudence of this line of action, indeed, was obvious; but, unfortunately, the Dodger, and Charley Bates, and Fagin, and Mr William Sikes, happened, one and all, to entertain a violent and deeply-rooted antipathy to going near a police office on any ground or pretext whatever.

However, the sudden entrance of the two young ladies whom Oliver had seen on a former occasion, caused the conversation to flow afresh.

"The very thing!" said Fagin. "Bet will go; won't you, my dear?"

"Wheres?" inquired the young lady.

"Only just up to the office, my dear," said the old man coaxingly.

The young lady expressed that she would not.

Fagin's countenance fell. He turned to the other female.

"Nancy, my dear," said the old man in a soothing manner, "what do *you* say?"

"That it won't do; so it's no use a-trying it on, Fagin," replied Nancy.

"What do you mean by that?" said Mr Sikes, looking up in a surly manner.

"What I say, Bill," replied the lady collectedly.

"Why, you're just the very person for it," reasoned Mr Sikes: "nobody about here knows anything of you."

"And as I don't want 'em to, neither," replied Nancy in the same composed manner, "it's rather more no than yes with me, Bill."

"She'll go, Fagin," said Sikes.

"No, she won't, Fagin," said Nancy.

"Yes, she will, Fagin," said Sikes.

And Mr Sikes was right. By dint of alternate threats, promises, and bribes, the lady in question was ultimately prevailed upon to undertake the commission.

CHAPTER 13

COMPRISING FURTHER PARTICULARS OF OLIVER'S STAY AT MR BROWNLOW'S, WITH THE REMARKABLE PREDICTION WHICH ONE MR GRIMWIG UTTERED CONCERNING HIM, WHEN HE WENT OUT ON AN ERRAND

Oliver soon recovering from the fainting-fit into which Mr Brownlow's abrupt exclamation had thrown him, the subject of the picture was carefully avoided, both by the old gentleman and Mrs Bedwin, in the conversation that ensued: which indeed bore no reference to Oliver's history or prospects, but was confined to such topics as might amuse without exciting him. He was still too weak to get up to breakfast; but, when he came down into the housekeeper's room next day, his first act was to cast an eager glance at the wall, in the hope of again looking on the face of the beautiful lady. His expectations were disappointed, however, for the picture had been removed.

"Ah!" said the housekeeper, watching the direction of Oliver's eyes. "It is gone, you see."

"I see it is ma'am," replied Oliver. "Why have they taken it away?"

"It has been taken down, child, because Mr Brownlow said, that as it seemed to worry you, perhaps it might prevent your getting well, you know," rejoined the old lady.

"Oh, no, indeed. It didn't worry me, ma'am," said Oliver. "I liked to see it. I quite loved it."

"Well, well!" said the old lady good-humouredly; "you get well as fast as ever you can, dear, and it shall be hung up again. There! I promise you that! Now, let us talk about something else."

One evening, about a week after the affair of the picture, as he was sitting talking to Mrs Bedwin, there came a message down from Mr Brownlow, that if Oliver Twist felt pretty well, he should like to see him in his study, and talk to him a little while.

Oliver tapped at the study door. On Mr Brownlow calling him to come in, he found himself in a little back room, quite full of books, with a window, looking into some pleasant little gardens. There was a table drawn up before the window, at which Mr Brownlow was seated reading.

"Now," said Mr Brownlow, speaking if possible in a kinder, but at the same time in a much more serious manner, than Oliver had ever known him assume yet, "I want you to pay great attention, my boy, to what I am going to say. I shall talk to you without any reserve; because I am sure you are as well able to understand me, as many older persons would be."

"Oh, don't tell me you are going to send me away, sir, pray!" exclaimed Oliver, alarmed at the serious tone of the old gentleman's commencement! "Don't turn me out of doors to wander in the streets again. Let me stay here, and be a servant. Don't send me back to the wretched place I came from. Have mercy upon a poor boy, sir!"

"My dear child," said the old gentleman, moved by the warmth of Oliver's sudden appeal; "you need not be afraid of my deserting you, unless you give me cause."

"I never, never will, sir," interposed Oliver.

"I hope not," rejoined the old gentleman. "I do not think you ever will."

As the old gentleman said this in a low voice: more to himself than to his companion: and as he remained silent for a short time afterwards: Oliver sat quite still.

"Well, well!" said the old gentleman at length, in a more cheerful tone, "I only say this, because you have a young heart; and knowing that I have suffered great pain and sorrow, you will be more careful, perhaps, not to wound me again. You say you are an orphan, without a friend in the world; all the inquiries I have been able to make, confirm the statement. Let me hear your story; where you come from; who brought you up; and how you got into the company in which I found you. Speak the truth, and you shall not be friendless while I live."

Oliver's sobs checked his utterance for some minutes; when he was on the point of beginning to relate how he had been brought up at the farm, and carried to the workhouse by Mr Bumble, a peculiarly impatient little double-knock was heard at the street-door: and the servant, running upstairs, announced Mr Grimwig.

"Is he coming up?" inquired Mr Brownlow.

"Yes, sir," replied the servant. "He asked if there were any muffins in the house; and, when I told him yes, he said he had come to tea."

Mr Brownlow smiled; and, turning to Oliver, said that Mr Grimwig was an old friend of his, and he must not mind his being a little rough in his manners; for he was a worthy creature at bottom, as he had reason to know.

"Shall I go downstairs, sir?" inquired Oliver.

"No," replied Mr Brownlow, "I would rather you remained here."

At this moment, there walked into the room: supporting himself by a thick stick: a stout old gentleman, rather lame in one leg, who was dressed in a blue coat, striped waistcoat, nankeen breeches and gaiters, and a broad-brimmed white hat, with the sides turned up with green. A very small-plaited shirt frill stuck out from his waistcoat; and a very long steel watch-chain, with nothing but a key at the end, dangled loosely below it.

"This is young Oliver Twist, whom we were speaking about," said Mr Brownlow.

Oliver bowed.

"You don't mean to say that's the boy who had the fever, I hope?" said Mr Grimwig, recoiling a little more.

"That is the boy," replied Mr Brownlow.

"How are you, boy?" said Mr Grimwig.

"A great deal better, thank you, sir," replied Oliver.

"And when are you going to hear a full, true, and particular account of the life and adventures of Oliver Twist?" asked Grimwig of Mr Brownlow.

"Tomorrow morning," replied Mr Brownlow. "I would rather he was alone with me at the time. Come up to me tomorrow morning at ten o'clock, my dear."

"Yes, sir," replied Oliver. He answered with some hesitation, because he was confused by Mr Grimwig's looking so hard at him.

"I'll tell you what," whispered that gentleman to Mr Brownlow; "he won't come up to you tomorrow morning. I saw him hesitate. He is deceiving you, my good friend."

"I'll swear he is not," replied Mr Brownlow, warmly.

"If he is not," said Mr Grimwig, "I'll—" and down went the stick.

"I'll answer for that boy's truth with my life!" said Mr Brownlow, knocking the table.

"And I for his falsehood with my head!" rejoined Mr Grimwig, knocking the table also.

"We shall see," said Mr Brownlow, checking his rising anger.

"We will," replied Mr Grimwig, with a provoking smile; "we will."

As fate would have it, Mrs Bedwin chanced to bring in, at this moment, a small parcel of books, which Mr Brownlow had that morning purchased of the identical book-stall keeper, who has already figured in this history; having laid them on the table, she prepared to leave the room.

"Stop the boy, Mrs Bedwin!" said Mr Brownlow; "there is something to go back."

"He has gone, sir," replied Mrs Bedwin.

"Call after him," said Mr Brownlow; "it's particular. He is a poor man, and they are not paid for. There are some books to be taken back, too."

"Send Oliver with them," said Mr Grimwig, with an ironical smile; "he will be sure to deliver them safely, you know."

"Yes; do let me take them, if you please, sir," said Oliver. "I'll run all the way, sir."

The old gentleman was just going to say that Oliver should not go out on any account; when a most malicious cough from Mr Grimwig determined him that he should; and that, by his prompt discharge of the commission, he should prove to him the injustice of his suspicions: on this head at least: at once.

"You *shall* go, my dear," said the old gentleman. "The books are on a chair by my table. Fetch them down."

Oliver, delighted to be of use, brought down the books under his arm in a great bustle; and waited, cap in hand, to hear what message he was to take.

"You are to say," said Mr Brownlow, glancing steadily at Grimwig; "you are to say that you have brought those books back; and that you have come to pay the four pound ten I owe him. This is a five-pound note, so you will have to bring me back, ten shillings change."

"I won't be ten minutes, sir," replied Oliver, eagerly. Having buttoned up the banknote in his jacket pocket, and placed the books carefully under his arm, he made a respectful bow, and left the room. Mrs Bedwin followed him to the street-door, giving him many directions about the nearest way, and the name of the bookseller, and the name of the street: all of which Oliver said he clearly understood. Having superadded many injunctions to be sure and not take cold, the old lady at length permitted him to depart.

"Bless his sweet face!" said the old lady, looking after him. "I can't bear, somehow, to let him go out of my sight."

At this moment, Oliver looked gaily round, and nodded before he turned the corner. The old lady smilingly returned his salutation, and, closing the door, went back to her own room.

"Let me see; he'll be back in twenty minutes, at the longest," said Mr Brownlow, pulling out his watch, and placing it on the table. "It will be dark by that time."

"Oh! you really expect him to come back, do you?" inquired Mr Grimwig.

"Don't you?" asked Mr Brownlow, smiling.

The spirit of contradiction was strong in Mr Grimwig's breast, at the moment; and it was rendered stronger by his friend's confident smile.

"No," he said, smiting the table with his fist, "I do not. The boy has a new suit of clothes on his back, a set of valuable books under his arm, and a five-pound note in his pocket. He'll join his old friends the thieves, and laugh at you. If ever that boy returns to this house, sir, I'll eat my head."

With these words he drew his chair closer to the table; and there the two friends sat, in silent expectation, with the watch between them.

It is worthy of remark, as illustrating the importance we attach to our own judgments, and the pride with which we put forth our most rash and hasty conclusions, that, although Mr Grimwig was not by any means a bad-hearted man, and though he would have been unfeignedly sorry to see his respected friend duped and deceived, he really did most earnestly and strongly hope at that moment, that Oliver Twist might not come back.

It grew so dark, that the figures on the dial-plate were scarcely discernible; but there the two old gentlemen continued to sit, in silence, with the watch between them.

CHAPTER 14

SHOWING HOW VERY FOND OF OLIVER TWIST THE MERRY OLD GENTLEMAN AND MISS NANCY WERE

In the obscure parlour of a low public-house, in the filthiest part of Little Saffron Hill; a dark and gloomy den, where a flaring gas-light burnt all day in the winter-time; and where no ray of sun ever shone in the summer: there sat, brooding over a little pewter measure and a small glass, strongly impregnated with the smell of liquor, a man in a velveteen coat, drab shorts, half-boots and stockings, who even by that dim light no experienced agent of the police would have hesitated to recognize as Mr William Sikes. At his feet sat a white-coated, red-eyed dog; who occupied himself, alternately, in winking at his master with both eyes at the same time; and in licking a large, fresh cut on one side of his mouth, which appeared to be the result of some recent conflict.

Meanwhile, Oliver Twist was on his way to the book-stall. When he got into Clerkenwell, he accidentally turned down a bye-street which was not exactly in his way; but not discovering his mistake until he had got halfway down it, and knowing it must lead in the right direction, he did not think it worth while to turn back; and so marched on, as quickly as he could, with the books under his arm.

He was walking along, thinking how happy and contented he ought to feel when he was startled by a young woman screaming out very loud, "Oh, my dear brother!" And he had hardly looked up, to see what the matter was, when he was stopped by having a pair of arms thrown tight round his neck.

"Don't," cried Oliver, struggling. "Let go of me. Who is it? What are you stopping me for?"

"Oh my gracious!" said the young woman, "Oh! Oliver! I've found him! Come home directly, you cruel boy! Come! He ran away, near a month ago, from his parents, who are hard-working and respectable people; and went and joined a set of thieves and bad characters; and almost broke his mother's heart."

"Young wretch!" said a woman.

"Go home, do, you little brute," said another.

"I am not," replied Oliver, greatly alarmed. "I don't know her. I haven't any sister, or father and mother either. I'm an orphan; I live at Pentonville."

"Only hear him, how he braves it out!" cried the young woman.

"Why, it's Nancy!" exclaimed Oliver; who now saw her face for the first time; and started back, in irrepressible astonishment.

"You see he knows me!" cried Nancy, appealing to the bystanders. "He can't help himself. Make him come home, there's good people, or he'll kill his dear mother and father, and break my heart!"

"What the devil's this?" said a man, bursting out of a beer-shop, with a white dog at his heels; "young Oliver! Come home to your poor mother, you young dog! Come home directly."

"I don't belong to them. I don't know them. Help! help!" cried Oliver, struggling in the man's powerful grasp.

"Help!" repeated the man. "Yes; I'll help you, you young rascal! What books are these? You've been a stealing 'em, have you? Give 'em here."

SHOEMAKER

With these words, the man tore the volumes from his grasp, and struck him on the head.

"That's right!" cried a looker-on, from a garret-window. "That's the only way of bringing him to his senses!"

"To be sure!" cried a sleepy-faced carpenter, casting an approving look at the garret-window.

"It'll do him good!" said the two women.

"And he shall have it, too!" rejoined the man, administering another blow, and seizing Oliver by the collar. "Come on, you young villain! Here, Bull's-eye, mind him, boy! Mind him!"

Weak with recent illness; stupefied by the blows and the suddenness of the attack; terrified by the fierce growling of the dog, and the brutality of the man; overpowered by the conviction of the bystanders that he really was the hardened little wretch he was described to be; what could one poor child do! Darkness had set in; it was a low neighborhood; no help was near; resistance was useless. In another moment he was dragged into a labyrinth of dark narrow courts, and was forced along them at a pace which rendered the few cries he dared to give utterance to, wholly unintelligible. It was of little moment, indeed, whether they were intelligible or no; for there was nobody to care for them, had they been ever so plain.

The gas-lamps were lighted; Mrs Bedwin was waiting anxiously at the open door; the servant had run up the street twenty times to see if there were any traces of Oliver; and still the two old gentlemen sat, perseveringly, in the dark parlour, with the watch between them.

CHAPTER 15

OLIVER'S DESTINY CONTINUING UNPROPITIOUS, BRINGS A GREAT MAN TO LONDON TO INJURE HIS REPUTATION

At six o'clock next morning, Mr Bumble: having exchanged his cocked hat for a round one, and encased his person in a blue great-coat with a cape to it, arrived in London.

Mr Bumble sat himself down in the house at which the coach stopped; and took a temperate dinner of steaks, oyster sauce, and porter. Putting a glass of hot gin-and-water on the chimney-piece, he drew his chair to the fire; and, with sundry moral reflections on the too-prevalent sin of discontent and complaining, composed himself to read the paper.

The very first paragraph upon which Mr Bumble's eye rested, was the following advertisement.

FIVE GUINEAS REWARD

Whereas a young boy, named

OLIVER TWIST,

absconded, or was enticed, on Thursday evening last, from his home, at Pentonville; and has not since been heard of.

The above reward will be paid to any person who will give such information as will lead to the discovery of the said Oliver Twist, or tend to throw any light upon his previous history, in which the advertiser is, for many reasons, warmly interested.

And then followed a full description of Oliver's dress, person, appearance, and disappearance: with the name and address of Mr Brownlow at full length.

Mr Bumble opened his eyes; read the advertisement, slowly and carefully, three several times; and in something more than five minutes was on his way to Pentonville: having actually, in his excitement, left the glass of hot gin-and-water, untasted.

"Is Mr Brownlow at home?" inquired Mr Bumble of the girl who opened the door.

To this inquiry the girl returned the not uncommon, but rather evasive reply of "I don't know; where do you come from?"

Mr Bumble no sooner uttered Oliver's name, in explanation of his errand, than Mrs Bedwin, who had been listening at the parlour door, hastened into the passage in a breathless state.

"Come in, come in," said the old lady: "I knew we should hear of him. Poor dear! I knew we should! I was certain of it! Bless his heart! I said so, all along."

Having said this, the worthy old lady hurried back into the parlour again; and seating herself on a sofa, burst into tears. The girl, who was not quite so susceptible, had run upstairs meanwhile; and now returned with a request that Mr Bumble would follow her immediately: which he did.

He was shown into the little back study, where sat Mr Brownlow and his friend Mr Grimwig, with decanters and glasses before them. The latter gentleman at once burst into the exclamation:

"A beadle. A parish beadle, or I'll eat my head."

"Pray don't interrupt just now," said Mr Brownlow. "Take a seat, will you?"

Mr Bumble sat himself down: quite confounded by the oddity of

Mr Grimwig's manner. Mr Brownlow moved the lamp, so as to obtain an uninterrupted view of the beadle's countenance; and said, with a little impatience,

"Now, sir, you come in consequence of having seen the advertisement?"

"Yes, sir," said Mr Bumble.

"And you *are* a beadle, are you not?" inquired Mr Grimwig.

"I am a porochial beadle, gentlemen," rejoined Mr Bumble, proudly.

"Of course," observed Mr Grimwig aside to his friend, "I knew he was. A beadle all over!"

Mr Brownlow gently shook his head to impose silence on his friend, and resumed:

"Do you know where this poor boy is now?"

"No more than nobody," replied Mr Bumble.

"Well, what *do* you know of him?" inquired the old gentleman. "Speak out, my friend, if you have anything to say. What *do* you know of him?"

"You don't happen to know any good of him, do you?" said Mr Grimwig, caustically; after an attentive perusal of Mr Bumble's features.

Mr Bumble, catching at the inquiry very quickly, shook his head with portentous solemnity.

"You see?" said Mr Grimwig, looking triumphantly at Mr Brownlow.

Mr Brownlow looked apprehensively at Mr Bumble's pursed-up countenance; and requested him to communicate what he knew regarding Oliver, in as few words as possible.

Mr Bumble put down his hat; unbuttoned his coat; folded his arms; inclined his head in a retrospective manner; and, after a few moments' reflection, commenced his story.

It would be tedious if given in the beadle's words: occupying, as it

did, some twenty minutes in the telling; but the sum and substance of it was, that Oliver was a foundling, born of low and vicious parents. That he had, from his birth, displayed no better qualities than treachery, ingratitude, and malice. That he had terminated his brief career in the place of his birth, by making a sanguinary and cowardly attack on an unoffending lad, and running away in the night-time from his master's house. In proof of his really being the person he represented himself, Mr Bumble laid upon the table the papers he had brought to town. Folding his arms again, he then awaited Mr Brownlow's observations.

"I fear it is all too true," said the old gentleman sorrowfully, after looking over the papers. "This is not much for your intelligence; but I would gladly have given you treble the money, if it had been favourable to the boy."

It is not improbable that if Mr Bumble had been possessed of this information at an earlier period of the interview, he might have imparted a very different colouring to his little history. It was too late to do it now, however; so he shook his head gravely, and, pocketing the five guineas, withdrew.

Mr Brownlow paced the room to and fro for some minutes; evidently so much disturbed by the beadle's tale, that even Mr Grimwig forbore to vex him further.

At length he stopped, and rang the bell violently.

"Mrs Bedwin," said Mr Brownlow, when the housekeeper appeared; "that boy, Oliver, is an imposter."

"It can't be, sir. It cannot be," said the old lady, energetically.

"I tell you he is," retorted the old gentleman. "What do you mean by can't be? We have just heard a full account of him from his birth; and he has been a thorough-paced little villain, all his life."

"I never will believe it, sir," replied the old lady, firmly. "Never!"

"You old women never believe anything but quack-doctors, and lying story-books," growled Mr Grimwig. "I knew it all along. Why didn't you take my advice in the beginning; you would, if he hadn't had a fever, I suppose, eh? He was interesting, wasn't he? Interesting! Bah!" And Mr Grimwig poked the fire with a flourish.

"He was a dear, grateful, gentle child, sir," retorted Mrs Bedwin, indignantly. "I know what children are, sir; and have done these forty years; and people who can't say the same, shouldn't say anything about them. That's my opinion!"

This was a hard hit at Mr Grimwig, who was a bachelor. As it extorted nothing from that gentleman but a smile, the old lady tossed her head, and smoothed down her apron preparatory to another speech, when she was stopped by Mr Brownlow.

"Silence!" said the old gentleman, feigning an anger he was far from feeling. "Never let me hear the boy's name again. I rang to tell you that. Never. Never, on any pretence, mind! You may leave the room, Mrs Bedwin. Remember! I am in earnest."

There were sad hearts at Mr Brownlow's that night.

Oliver's heart sank within him, when he thought of his good kind friends; it was well for him that he could not know what they had heard, or it might have broken outright.

CHAPTER 16

IN WHICH A NOTABLE PLAN IS DISCUSSED AND DETERMINED ON

It was a chill, damp, windy night, when Fagin: buttoning his great-coat tight round his shrivelled body, and pulling the collar up over his ears so as completely to obscure the lower part of his face: emerged from his den. He paused on the step as the door was locked and chained behind him; and having listened while the boys made all secure, and until their retreating footsteps were no longer audible, slunk down the street as quickly as he could.

He kept on his course, through many winding and narrow ways, until he reached Bethnal Green; then, turning suddenly off to the left, he soon became involved in a maze of the mean and dirty streets which abound in that close and densely-populated quarter.

The old man was evidently too familiar with the ground he traversed to be at all bewildered, either by the darkness of the night, or the intricacies of the way. He hurried through several alleys and streets, and at length turned into one, lighted only by a single lamp at the farther end. At the door of a house in this street, he knocked; and having exchanged a few muttered words with the person who opened it, he walked upstairs.

A dog growled as he touched the handle of a room-door; and a man's voice demanded who was there.

"Only me, Bill; only me, my dear," said the old man, looking in.

"Bring in your body then," said Sikes. "Lie down, you stupid brute! Don't you know the devil when he's got a great-coat on?"

Apparently, the dog had been somewhat deceived by Mr Fagin's outer garment; for as the old man unbuttoned it, and threw it over the back of a chair, he retired to the corner from which he had risen: wagging his tail as he went, to show that he was as well satisfied as it was in his nature to be.

"Well!" said Sikes.

"Well, my dear," replied the old man. "Ah! Nancy."

Nancy quickly brought a bottle from a cupboard, in which there were many: which, to judge from the diversity of their appearance, were filled with several kinds of liquids. Sikes, pouring out a glass of brandy, bade the old man drink it off.

"About that crib at Chertsey, Bill?" said the old man, drawing his chair forward, and speaking in a very low voice.

"Yes. Wot about it?" inquired Sikes.

"Ah, you know what I mean, my dear," said the old man. "He knows what I mean, Nancy; don't he?"

"No, he don't," sneered Mr Sikes. "Or he won't, and that's the same thing. Speak out, and call things by their right names; don't sit there, winking and blinking, and talking to me in hints, as if you warn't the very first that thought about the robbery. What d'ye mean?"

"There, there," said the old man coaxingly. "It was only my caution, nothing more. Now, my dear, about that crib at Chertsey; when is it to be done, Bill, eh? When is it to be done? Such plate, my dear, such plate!"

said the old man: rubbing his hands, and elevating his eyebrows in a rapture of anticipation.

"Not at all," replied Sikes coldly.

"Not to be done at all!" echoed the old man, leaning back in his chair.

"No, not at all," rejoined Sikes. "At least it can't be a put-up job, as we expected."

"Then it hasn't been properly gone about," said the old man, turning pale with anger. "Don't tell me!"

A long silence ensued; during which Fagin was plunged in deep thought, with his face wrinkled into an expression of villany perfectly demoniacal. Sikes eyed him furtively from time to time. Nancy, apparently fearful of irritating the housebreaker, sat with her eyes fixed upon the fire, as if she had been deaf to all that passed.

"Fagin," said Sikes, abruptly breaking the stillness that prevailed; "is it worth fifty shiners extra, if it's safely done from the outside?"

"Yes," said the old man, as suddenly rousing himself.

"Is it a bargain?" inquired Sikes.

"Yes, my dear, yes," rejoined the old man; his eyes glistening, and every muscle in his face working, with the excitement that the inquiry had awakened.

"Then," said Sikes, thrusting aside the old man's hand, with some disdain, "let it come off as soon as you like. Toby and me were over the garden-wall the night afore last, sounding the panels of the door and shutters. The crib's barred up at night like a jail; but there's one part we can crack, safe and softly."

"Which is that, Bill?" asked the old man eagerly.

"Why," whispered Sikes, "as you cross the lawn—"

"Yes?" said the old man, bending his head forward, with his eyes almost starting out of it.

"Umph!" cried Sikes, stopping short, as the girl, scarcely moving her head, looked suddenly round, and pointed for an instant to the old man's face. "Never mind which part it is. You can't do it without me, I know; but it's best to be on the safe side when one deals with you."

"As you like, my dear, as you like," replied the old man. "Is there no help wanted, but yours and Toby's?"

"None," said Sikes. "'Cept a centre-bit and a boy. The first we've both got; the second you must find us."

"A boy!" exclaimed the old man. "Oh! then it's a panel, eh?"

"Never mind wot it is!" replied Sikes. "I want a boy, and he mustn't be a big 'un."

The old man nodded his head towards Nancy, who was still gazing at the fire; and intimated, by a sign, that he would have her told to leave the room. Sikes shrugged his shoulders impatiently, as if he thought the precaution unnecessary; but complied, nevertheless, by requesting Miss Nancy to fetch him a jug of beer.

"You don't want any beer," said Nancy, folding her arms, and retaining her seat very composedly.

"I tell you I do!" replied Sikes.

"Nonsense," rejoined the girl coolly. "Go on, Fagin. I know what he's going to say, Bill; he needn't mind me."

The old man still hesitated. Sikes looked from one to the other in some surprise.

"Why, you don't mind the old girl, do you, Fagin?" he asked at length. "You've known her long enough to trust her, or the Devil's in it. She ain't one to blab. Are you, Nancy?"

"*I* should think not!" replied the young lady: drawing her chair up to the table, and putting her elbows upon it.

"No, no, my dear, I know you're not," said the old man; "but—" and again the old man paused.

"But wot?" inquired Sikes.

"I didn't know whether she mightn't p'r'aps be out of sorts, you know, my dear, replied the old man.

At this, Miss Nancy burst into a loud laugh; and, swallowing a glass of brandy, shook her head with an air of defiance, and burst into sundry exclamations of "Keep the game a-going!" "Never say die!" and the like. These seemed to have the effect of reassuring both gentlemen; for the old man nodded his head with a satisfied air, and resumed his seat: as did Mr Sikes likewise.

"Now, Fagin," said Nancy with a laugh. "Tell Bill at once, about Oliver!"

"Ha! you're a clever one, my dear; the sharpest girl I ever saw!" said the old man, patting her on the neck. "It *was* about Oliver I was going to speak, sure enough. Ha! ha! ha!"

"What about him?" demanded Sikes.

"He's the boy for you, my dear," replied the old man in a hoarse whisper; laying his finger on the side of his nose, and grinning frightfully.

"He!" exclaimed Sikes.

"Have him, Bill!" said Nancy. "I would, if I was in your place. He mayn't be so much up, as any of the others; but that's not what you want, if he's only to open a door for you. Depend upon it he's a safe one, Bill."

"I know he is," rejoined Fagin. "He's been in good training these last few weeks, and it's time he began to work for his bread. Besides, the others are all too big."

"Well, he is just the size I want," said Mr Sikes, ruminating.

"And will do everything you want, Bill, my dear," interposed the old man; "he can't help himself. That is, if you frighten him enough."

"Frighten him!" echoed Sikes. "It'll be no sham frightening, mind you. If there's anything queer about him when we once get into the work; in for a penny, in for a pound. You won't see him alive again, Fagin. Think of that, before you send him. Mark my words!" said the robber, poising a crowbar, which he had drawn from under the bedstead.

"I've thought of it all," said the old man with energy. "I've – I've had my eye upon him, my dears, close – close. Once let him feel that he is one of us; once fill his mind with the idea that he has been a thief; and he's ours! Ours for his life. Oho! It couldn't have come about better!" The old man crossed his arms upon his breast; and, drawing his head and shoulders into a heap, literally hugged himself for joy.

"Ours!" said Sikes. "Yours, you mean."

"Perhaps I do, my dear," said the old man, with a shrill chuckle. "Mine, if you like, Bill."

After some discussion, in which all three took an active part, it was decided that Nancy should repair to the old man's next evening when the night had set in, and bring Oliver away with her.

CHAPTER 17

WHEREIN OLIVER IS DELIVERED OVER TO MR WILLIAM SIKES

When Oliver awoke in the morning, he was a good deal surprised to find that a new pair of shoes, with strong thick soles, had been placed at his bedside; and that his old shoes had been removed. At first, he was pleased with the discovery: hoping that it might be the forerunner of his release; but such thoughts were quickly dispelled, on his sitting down to breakfast along with Fagin, who told him, in a tone and manner which increased his alarm, that he was to be taken to the residence of Bill Sikes that night.

"To – to – stop there, sir?" asked Oliver, anxiously.

"No, no, my dear. Not to stop there," replied the old man. "We shouldn't like to lose you. Don't be afraid, Oliver, you shall come back to us again. Ha! ha! ha! We won't be so cruel as to send you away, my dear. Oh no, no!"

Fagin, who was stooping over the fire toasting a piece of bread, looked round as he bantered Oliver thus; and chuckled as if to show that he knew he would still be very glad to get away if he could.

"I suppose," said the old man, fixing his eyes on Oliver, "you want to know what you're going to Bill's for – eh, my dear?"

Oliver coloured, involuntarily, to find that the old thief had been reading his thoughts; but boldly said, Yes, he did want to know.

"Why, do you think?" inquired Fagin, parrying the question.

"Indeed I don't know, sir," replied Oliver.

"Bah!" said the old man, turning away with a disappointed countenance from a close perusal of the boy's face. "Wait till Bill tells you, then."

The old man seemed much vexed by Oliver's not expressing any greater curiosity on the subject; but the truth is, that, although Oliver felt very anxious, he was too much confused by the earnest cunning of Fagin's looks, and his own speculations, to make any further inquiries just then. He had no other opportunity: for the old man remained very surly and silent till night: when he prepared to go abroad.

"You may burn a candle," said the old man, putting one upon the table. "And here's a book for you to read, till they come to fetch you. Goodnight!"

"Goodnight!" replied Oliver, softly.

The old man walked to the door: looking over his shoulder at the boy as he went.

Oliver leaned his head upon his hand when the old man disappeared, and pondered, with a trembling heart.

With a heavy sigh, he snuffed the candle, and, taking up the book which Fagin had left with him, began to read, when a rustling noise aroused him.

"What's that!" he cried, starting up, and catching sight of a figure standing by the door. "Who's there?"

"Me. Only me," replied a tremulous voice.

Oliver raised the candle above his head: and looked towards the door. It was Nancy.

"Put down the light," said the girl, turning away her head. "It hurts my eyes."

Oliver saw that she was very pale, and gently inquired if she were ill. The girl threw herself into a chair, with her back towards him: and wrung her hands; but made no reply.

"God forgive me!" she cried after a while, "I never thought of this."

"Has anything happened?" asked Oliver. "Can I help you? I will if I can."

"Hush!" said the girl, stooping over him, and pointing to the door as she looked cautiously round. "You can't help yourself. I have tried hard for you, but all to no purpose. You are hedged round and round. If ever you are to get loose from here, this is not the time."

Struck by the energy of her manner, Oliver looked up in her face with great surprise. She seemed to speak the truth; her countenance was white and agitated; and she trembled with very earnestness.

"I have saved you from being ill-used once, and I will again, and I do now," continued the girl aloud; "for those who would have fetched you, if I had not, would have been far more rough than me. I have promised for your being quiet and silent; if you are not, you will only do harm to yourself and me too, and perhaps be my death. See here! I have borne all this for you already, as true as God sees me show it."

She pointed, hastily, to some livid bruises on her neck and arms; and continued, with great rapidity:

"Remember this! And don't let me suffer more for you, just now. If I could help you, I would; but I have not the power. They don't mean to harm you; whatever they make you do, is no fault of yours. Hush! Every word from you is a blow for me. Give me your hand. Make haste! Your hand!"

She caught the hand which Oliver instinctively placed in hers, and, blowing out the light, drew him after her up the stairs. The door was opened, quickly, by someone shrouded in the darkness, and was as quickly closed, when they had passed out. A hackney-cabriolet was in waiting; with the same vehemence which she had exhibited in addressing Oliver, the girl pulled him in with her, and drew the curtains close. The driver wanted no directions, but lashed his horse into full speed, without the delay of an instant.

The girl still held Oliver fast by the hand, and continued to pour into his ear, the warnings and assurances she had already imparted. All was so quick and hurried, that he had scarcely time to recollect where he was, or how he came there, when the carriage stopped at the house to which the old man's steps had been directed on the previous evening.

For one brief moment, Oliver cast a hurried glance along the empty street, and a cry for help hung upon his lips. But the girl's voice was in his ear, beseeching him in such tones of agony to remember her, that he had

not the heart to utter it. While he hesitated, the opportunity was gone; he was already in the house, and the door was shut.

"This way," said the girl, releasing her hold for the first time. "Bill!"

"Hallo!" replied Sikes: appearing at the head of the stairs, with a candle. "Oh! That's the time of day. Come on!"

This was a very strong expression of approbation, an uncommonly hearty welcome, from a person of Mr Sikes' temperament. Nancy, appearing much gratified thereby, saluted him cordially.

"Bull's-eye's gone home with Tom," observed Sikes, as he lighted them up. "He'd have been in the way."

"That's right," rejoined Nancy.

"So you've got the kid," said Sikes, when they had all reached the room: closing the door as he spoke.

"Yes, here he is," replied Nancy.

"Did he come quiet?" inquired Sikes.

"Like a lamb," rejoined Nancy.

"I'm glad to hear it," said Sikes, looking grimly at Oliver; "for the sake of his young carcase: as would otherways have suffered for it. Come here, young 'un; and let me read you a lectur', which is as well got over at once."

Thus addressing his new pupil, Mr Sikes pulled off Oliver's cap and threw it into a corner; and then, taking him by the shoulder, sat himself down by the table, and stood the boy in front of him.

"Now, first: do you know wot this is?" inquired Sikes, taking up a pocket-pistol which lay on the table.

Oliver replied in the affirmative.

"Well, then, look here," continued Sikes. "This is powder; that 'ere's a bullet; and this is a little bit of a old hat for waddin'."

Oliver murmured his comprehension of the different bodies referred to; and Mr Sikes proceeded to load the pistol, with great nicety and deliberation.

"Now it's loaded," said Mr Sikes, when he had finished.

"Yes, I see it is, sir," replied Oliver.

"Well," said the robber, grasping Oliver's wrist, and putting the barrel so close to his temple that they touched; at which moment the boy could not repress a start; "if you speak a word when you're out o' doors with me, except when I speak to you, that loading will be in your head without notice. So, if you *do* make up your mind to speak without leave, say your prayers first."

Having bestowed a scowl upon the object of this warning, to increase its effect, Mr Sikes continued.

"As near as I know, there isn't anybody as would be asking very partickler arter you, if you *was* disposed of; so I needn't take this devil-and-all of trouble to explain matters to you, if it warn't for your own good. D'ye hear me?"

"The short and the long of what you mean," said Nancy: speaking very emphatically, and slightly frowning at Oliver as if to bespeak his serious attention to her words: "is, that if you're crossed by him in this job you have on hand, you'll prevent his ever telling tales afterwards, by shooting him through the head, and will take your chance of swinging for it, as you do for a great many other things in the way of business, every month of your life."

"That's it!" observed Mr Sikes, approvingly; "women can always put things in fewest words – except when it's blowing up; and then they lengthens it out. And now that he's thoroughly up to it, let's have some supper, and get a snooze before starting."

Supper being ended – it may be easily conceived that Oliver had no great appetite for it – Mr Sikes disposed of a couple of glasses of spirits and water, and threw himself on the bed; ordering Nancy, with many imprecations in case of failure, to call him at five precisely. Oliver stretched himself in his clothes, by command of the same authority, on a mattress upon the floor; and the girl, mending the fire, sat before it, in readiness to rouse them at the appointed time.

For a long time Oliver lay awake, thinking it not impossible that Nancy might seek that opportunity of whispering some further advice; but the girl sat brooding over the fire, without moving, save now and then to trim the light. Weary with watching and anxiety, he at length fell asleep.

When he awoke, the table was covered with tea-things, and Sikes was thrusting various articles into the pockets of his great-coat, which hung over the back of a chair. Nancy was busily engaged in preparing breakfast.

It was not yet daylight; for the candle was still burning, and it was quite dark outside. A sharp rain, too, was beating against the window-panes; and the sky looked black and cloudy.

"Now, then!" growled Sikes, as Oliver started up; "half past five! Look sharp, or you'll get no breakfast; for it's late as it is."

Oliver was not long in making his toilet; having taken some breakfast, he replied to a surly inquiry from Sikes, by saying that he was quite ready.

Nancy, scarcely looking at the boy, threw him a handkerchief to tie round his throat; Sikes gave him a large rough cape to button over his shoulders. Thus attired, he gave his hand to the robber, who, merely pausing to show him with a menacing gesture that he had that same pistol in a side-pocket of his great-coat, clasped it firmly in his, and, exchanging a farewell with Nancy, led him away.

Oliver turned, for an instant, when they reached the door, in the hope of meeting a look from the girl. But she had resumed her old seat in front of the fire, and sat perfectly motionless before it.

CHAPTER 18

THE EXPEDITION

It was a cheerless morning when they got into the street; blowing and raining hard; and the clouds looking dull and stormy.

By the time they had turned into the Bethnal Green Road, the day had fairly begun to break. Many of the lamps were already extinguished; a few country waggons were slowly toiling on, towards London; now and then, a stagecoach, covered with mud, rattled briskly by.

Turning down Sun Street and Crown Street, and crossing Finsbury Square, Mr Sikes struck, by way of Chiswell Street, into Barbican: thence into Long Lane, and so into Smithfield; from which latter place arose a tumult of discordant sounds that filled Oliver Twist with amazement.

They held their course at this rate, until they had passed Hyde Park corner, and were on their way to Kensington: when Sikes relaxed his pace, until an empty cart, which was at some little distance behind, came up. Seeing "Hounslow" written on it, he asked the driver with as much civility as he could assume, if he would give them a lift as far as Isleworth.

"Jump up," said the man. "Is that your boy?"

"Yes; he's my boy," replied Sikes, looking hard at Oliver, and putting his hand abstractedly into the pocket where the pistol was.

"Your father walks rather too quick for you, don't he, my man?"

inquired the driver: seeing that Oliver was out of breath.

"Not a bit of it," replied Sikes, interposing. "He's used to it. Here, take hold of my hand, Ned. In with you!"

Thus addressing Oliver, he helped him into the cart; and the driver, pointing to a heap of sacks, told him to lie down there, and rest himself.

As they passed the different milestones, Oliver wondered, more and more, where his companion meant to take him. Kensington, Hammersmith, Chiswick, Kew Bridge, Brentford, were all passed; and yet they went on as steadily as if they had only just begun their journey. At length, they came to a public-house called the Coach and Horses: a little way beyond which, another road appeared to turn off. And here, the cart stopped.

Sikes dismounted with great precipitation, holding Oliver by the hand all the while; and lifting him down directly, bestowed a furious look upon him, and rapped the side-pocket with his fist, in a significant manner.

"Goodbye, boy," said the man.

"He's sulky," replied Sikes, giving him a shake; "he's sulky. A young dog! Don't mind him."

"Not I!" rejoined the other, getting into his cart. "It's a fine day, after all." And he drove away.

Sikes waited until he had fairly gone; and then, telling Oliver he might look about him if he wanted, once again led him onward on his journey.

They turned round to the left, a short way past the public-house; and then, taking a right-hand road, walked on for a long time: passing many large gardens and gentlemen's houses on both sides of the way, and stopping for nothing but a little beer, until they reached a town. Here against the wall of a house, Oliver saw written up in pretty large letters, "Hampton." They lingered about, in the fields, for some hours. At length, they came back into the town; and, turning into an old public-house with a defaced sign-board, ordered some dinner by the kitchen fire.

They had some cold meat for dinner, and sat so long after it, while Mr Sikes indulged himself with three or four pipes, that Oliver began to feel quite certain they were not going any further. Being much tired with the walk, and getting up so early, he dozed a little at first; then, quite overpowered by fatigue and the fumes of the tobacco, fell asleep.

It was quite dark when he was awakened by a push from Sikes. Rousing himself sufficiently to sit up and look about him, he found that worthy in close fellowship and communication with a labouring man, over a pint of ale.

"So, you're going on to Lower Halliford, are you?" inquired Sikes.

"Yes, I am," replied the man, who seemed a little the worse – or better, as the case might be – for drinking; "and not slow about it neither. My horse hasn't got a load behind him going back, as he had coming up in the mornin'; and he won't be long a-doing of it. Here's luck to him. Ecod! he's a good 'un!"

"Could you give my boy and me a lift as far as there?" demanded Sikes, pushing the ale towards his new friend.

"If you're going directly, I can," replied the man, looking out of the pot. "Are you going to Halliford?"

"Going on to Shepperton," replied Sikes.

"I'm your man, as far as I go," replied the other. "Is all paid, Becky?"

"Yes, the other gentleman's paid," replied the girl.

"I say!" said the man, with tipsy gravity; "that won't do, you know."

"Why not?" rejoined Sikes. "You're a-going to accommodate us, and wot's to prevent my standing treat for a pint or so, in return?"

The stranger reflected upon this argument, with a very profound face;

having done so, he seized Sikes by the hand and declared he was a real good fellow. To which Mr Sikes replied, he was joking; as, if he had been sober, there would have been strong reason to suppose he was.

After the exchange of a few more compliments, they bade the company goodnight, and went out; the girl gathering up the pots and glasses as they did so, and lounging out to the door, with her hands full, to see the party start.

As they passed Sunbury Church, the clock struck seven.

Sunbury was passed through, and they came again into the lonely road. Two or three miles more, and the cart stopped. Sikes alighted, took Oliver by the hand, and they once again walked on.

They turned into no house at Shepperton, as the weary boy had expected; but still kept walking on, in mud and darkness, through gloomy lanes and over cold open wastes, until they came within sight of the lights of a town at no great distance. On looking intently forward, Oliver saw that the water was just below them, and that they were coming to the foot of a bridge.

Sikes kept straight on, until they were close upon the bridge; then turned suddenly down a bank upon the left.

"The water!" thought Oliver, turning sick with fear. "He has brought me to this lonely place to murder me!"

He was about to throw himself on the ground, and make one struggle for his young life, when he saw that they stood before a solitary house: all ruinous and decayed. There was a window on each side of the dilapidated entrance; and one story above; but no light was visible. The house was dark, dismantled: and, to all appearance, uninhabited.

Sikes, with Oliver's hand still in his, softly approached the low porch, and raised the latch. The door yielded to the pressure, and they passed in together.

CHAPTER 19

THE BURGLARY

"Hallo!" cried a loud, hoarse voice, as soon as they set foot in the passage.

"Don't make such a row," said Sikes, bolting the door. "Show a glim, Toby."

"Aha! my pal!" cried the same voice. "A glim, Barney, a glim! Show the gentleman in, Barney; wake up first, if convenient."

The speaker appeared to throw a boot-jack, or some such article, at the person he addressed, to rouse him from his slumbers: for the noise of a wooden body, falling violently, was heard; and then an indistinct muttering, as of a man between sleep and awake.

Sikes pushed Oliver before him; and they entered a low dark room with a smoky fire, two or three broken chairs, a table, and a very old couch: on which, with his legs much higher than his head, a man was reposing at full length, smoking a long clay pipe. He was dressed in a smartly-cut snuff-coloured coat, with large brass buttons; an orange neckerchief; a coarse, staring, shawl-pattern waistcoat; and drab breeches. Mr Crackit (for he it was) had no very great quantity of hair, either upon his head or face; but what he had, was of a reddish dye, and tortured into long corkscrew curls, through which he occasionally thrust some very dirty fingers, ornamented with large common rings.

"Bill, my boy!" said this figure, turning his head towards the door, "I'm glad to see you. Hallo!"

Uttering this exclamation in a tone of great surprise, as his eyes rested on Oliver, Mr Toby Crackit brought himself into a sitting posture, and demanded who that was.

"The boy. Only the boy!" replied Sikes, drawing a chair towards the fire; and stooping over his recumbent friend, he whispered a few words in his ear: at which Mr Crackit laughed immensely, and honoured Oliver with a long stare of astonishment.

"Now," said Sikes, as he resumed his seat, "if you'll give us something to eat and drink while we're waiting, you'll put some heart in us; or in me, at all events. Sit down by the fire, younker, and rest yourself; for you'll have to go out with us again tonight, though not very far off."

This done, and Sikes having satisfied his appetite (Oliver could eat nothing but a small crust of bread which they made him swallow), the two men laid themselves down on chairs for a short nap. Oliver retained his stool by the fire; Barney, wrapped in a blanket, stretched himself on the floor: close outside the fender.

They slept, or appeared to sleep, for some time; nobody stirring but Barney, who rose once or twice to throw coals upon the fire. Oliver fell into a heavy doze: imagining himself straying along the gloomy lanes, or wandering about the dark churchyard, or retracing some one or other of the scenes of the past day: when he was roused by Toby Crackit jumping up and declaring it was half-past one.

In an instant, the other two were on their legs, and all were actively engaged in busy preparation. Sikes and his companion enveloped their necks and chins in large dark shawls, and drew on their great-coats; while Barney, opening a cupboard, brought forth several articles, which he hastily crammed into the pockets.

"Barkers for me, Barney," said Toby Crackit.

"Here they are," replied Barney, producing a pair of pistols. "You loaded them yourself."

"All right!" replied Toby, stowing them away. "The persuaders?"

"I've got 'em," replied Sikes.

"Crape, keys, centre-bits, darkies – nothing forgotten?" inquired Toby: fastening a small crowbar to a loop inside the skirt of his coat.

"All right," rejoined his companion. "Bring them bits of timber, Barney. That's the time of day."

With these words, he took a thick stick from Barney's hands, who, having delivered another to Toby, busied himself in fastening on Oliver's cape.

"Now then!" said Sikes, holding out his hand.

Oliver: who was completely stupefied by the unwonted exercise, and the air: put his hand mechanically into that which Sikes extended for the purpose.

"Take his other hand, Toby," said Sikes. "Look out, Barney."

The man went to the door, and returned to announce that all was quiet. The two robbers issued forth with Oliver between them. Barney, having made all fast, rolled himself up as before, and was soon asleep again.

It was now intensely dark. The fog was much heavier than it had been in the early part of the night; and the atmosphere was so damp, that, although no rain fell, Oliver's hair and eyebrows, within a few minutes after leaving the house, had become stiff with the half-frozen moisture that was floating about. They crossed the bridge, and kept on towards the lights which he had seen before. They were at no great distance off; and, as they walked pretty briskly, they soon arrived at Chertsey.

"Slap through the town," whispered Sikes; "there'll be nobody in the way, tonight, to see us."

Toby acquiesced; and they hurried through the main street of the little town, which at that late hour was wholly deserted. A dim light shone at intervals from some bedroom window; and the hoarse barking of dogs occasionally broke the silence of the night. But there was nobody abroad. They had cleared the town, as the church bell struck two.

Quickening their pace, they turned up a road upon the left hand. After walking about a quarter of a mile, they stopped before a detached house surrounded by a wall: to the top of which, Toby Crackit, scarcely pausing to take breath, climbed in a twinkling.

"The boy next," said Toby. "Hoist him up; I'll catch hold of him."

Before Oliver had time to look round, Sikes had caught him under the arms; and in three or four seconds he and Toby were lying on the grass on the other side. Sikes followed directly. And they stole cautiously towards the house.

And now, for the first time, Oliver, well-nigh mad with grief and terror, saw that housebreaking and robbery, if not murder, were the objects of the expedition. He clasped his hands together, and involuntarily uttered a subdued exclamation of horror. A mist came before his eyes; the cold sweat stood upon his ashy face; his limbs failed him; and he sank upon his knees.

"Get up!" murmured Sikes, trembling with rage, and drawing the pistol from his pocket; "Get up, or I'll strew your brains upon the grass."

"Oh! for God's sake let me go!" cried Oliver; "let me run away and die in the fields. I will never come near London; never, never! Oh! pray have mercy on me, and do not make me steal. For the love of all the bright Angels that rest in Heaven, have mercy upon me!"

The man to whom this appeal was made, swore a dreadful oath, and had cocked the pistol, when Toby, striking it from his grasp, placed his hand upon the boy's mouth, and dragged him to the house.

"Hush!" cried the man; "it won't answer here. Say another word, and I'll do your business myself with a crack on the head. That makes no noise, and is quite as certain, and more genteel. Here, Bill, wrench the shutter open. He's game enough now, I'll engage. I've seen older hands of his age took the same way, for a minute or two, on a cold night."

Sikes, invoking terrific imprecations upon Fagin's head for sending Oliver on such an errand, plied the crowbar vigorously, but with little noise. After some delay, and some assistance from Toby, the shutter to which he had referred, swung open on its hinges.

It was a little lattice window, about five feet and a half above the ground, at the back of the house: which belonged to a scullery, or small brewing-place, at the end of the passage. The aperture was so small, that the inmates had probably not thought it worth while to defend it more securely; but it was large enough to admit a boy of Oliver's size, nevertheless. A very brief exercise of Mr Sikes' art, sufficed to overcome the fastening of the lattice; and it soon stood wide open also.

"Now listen, you young limb," whispered Sikes, drawing a dark lantern from his pocket, and throwing the glare full on Oliver's face; "I'm a going to put you through there. Take this light; go softly up the steps straight afore you, and along the little hall, to the street door; unfasten it, and let us in."

"There's a bolt at the top, you won't be able to reach," interposed Toby. "Stand upon one of the hall chairs. There are three there, Bill, with a jolly large blue unicorn and gold pitchfork on 'em: which is the old lady's arms."

"Keep quiet, can't you?" replied Sikes, with a threatening look. "The room-door is open, is it?"

"Wide," replied Toby, after peeping in to satisfy himself. "The game of that is, that they always leave it open with a catch, so that the dog, who's got a bed in here, may walk up and down the passage when he feels wakeful. Ha! ha! Barney 'ticed him away tonight. So neat!"

Although Mr Crackit spoke in a scarcely audible whisper, and laughed without noise, Sikes imperiously commanded him to be silent, and to get to work. Toby complied, by first producing his lantern, and placing it on the ground; then by planting himself firmly with his head against the wall beneath the window, and his hands upon his knees, so as to make a step of his back. This was no sooner done, than Sikes, mounting upon him, put Oliver gently through the window with his feet first; and, without leaving hold of his collar, planted him safely on the floor inside.

"Take this lantern," said Sikes, looking into the room. "You see the stairs afore you?"

Oliver, more dead than alive, gasped out "Yes." Sikes, pointing to the street-door with the pistol-barrel, briefly advised him to take notice that he was within shot all the way; and that if he faltered, he would fall dead that instant.

"It's done in a minute," said Sikes, in the same low whisper. "Directly I leave go of you, do your work. Hark!"

"What's that?" whispered the other man.

They listened intently.

"Nothing," said Sikes, releasing his hold of Oliver. "Now!"

In the short time he had had to collect his senses, the boy had firmly resolved that, whether he died in the attempt or not, he would make one effort to dart upstairs from the hall, and alarm the family. Filled with this idea, he advanced at once, but stealthily.

"Come back!" suddenly cried Sikes aloud. "Back! back!"

Scared by the sudden breaking of the dead stillness of the place, and by a loud cry which followed it, Oliver let his lantern fall, and knew not whether to advance or fly.

The cry was repeated – a light appeared – a vision of two terrified half-dressed men at the top of the stairs swam before his eyes – a flash – a loud noise – a smoke – a crash somewhere, but where he knew not – and he staggered back.

Sikes had disappeared for an instant; but he was up again, and had him by the collar before the smoke had cleared away. He fired his own pistol after the men, who were already retreating; and dragged the boy up.

"Clasp your arm tighter," said Sikes, as he drew him through the window. "Give me a shawl here. They've hit him. Quick! How the boy bleeds!"

Then came the loud ringing of a bell, mingled with the noise of fire-arms, and the shouts of men, and the sensation of being carried over uneven ground at a rapid pace. And then, the noises grew confused in the distance; and a cold deadly feeling crept over the boy's heart; and he saw or heard no more.

CHAPTER 20

WHICH CONTAINS THE SUBSTANCE OF A PLEASANT CONVERSATION BETWEEN MR BUMBLE AND A LADY; AND SHOWS THAT EVEN A BEADLE MAY BE SUSCEPTIBLE ON SOME POINTS

Mrs Corney, the matron of the workhouse to which our readers have been already introduced as the birthplace of Oliver Twist, sat herself down before a cheerful fire in her own little room, and glanced, with no small degree of complacency, at a small round table: on which stood a tray of corresponding size, furnished with all necessary materials for the most grateful meal that matrons enjoy. In fact, Mrs Corney was about to solace herself with a cup of tea.

"Well!" said the matron, leaning her elbow on the table, and looking reflectively at the fire; "I'm sure we have all on us a great deal to be grateful for! A great deal, if we did but know it. Ah!"

With these words, the matron dropped into her chair, and, once more resting her elbow on the table, thought of her solitary fate. The small teapot, and the single cup, had awakened in her mind sad recollections of Mr Corney (who had not been dead more than five-and-twenty years); and she was overpowered.

"I shall never get another!" said Mrs Corney, pettishly; "I shall never

get another – like him."

Whether this remark bore reference to the husband, or the teapot, is uncertain. It might have been the latter; for Mrs Corney looked at it as she spoke; and took it up afterwards. She had just tasted her first cup, when she was disturbed by a soft tap at the room-door.

"Oh, come in with you!" said Mrs Corney, sharply. "Some of the old women dying, I suppose. They always die when I'm at meals. Don't stand there, letting the cold air in, don't. What's amiss now, eh?"

"Nothing, ma'am, nothing," replied a man's voice.

"Dear me!" exclaimed the matron, in a much sweeter tone, "is that Mr Bumble?"

"At your service, ma'am," said Mr Bumble, who had been stopping outside to rub his shoes clean, and to shake the snow off his coat; and who now made his appearance, bearing the cocked hat in one hand and a bundle in the other. "Shall I shut the door, ma'am?"

The lady modestly hesitated to reply, lest there should be any impropriety in holding an interview with Mr Bumble, with closed doors. Mr Bumble taking advantage of the hesitation, and being very cold himself, shut it without permission.

"Hard weather, Mr Bumble," said the matron.

"Hard, indeed, ma'am," replied the beadle.

"If you please, mistress," said a withered old female pauper, hideously ugly: putting her head in at the door, "Old Sally is a-going fast."

"Well, what's that to me?" angrily demanded the matron. "I can't keep her alive, can I?"

"No, no, mistress," replied the old woman, "nobody can; she's far beyond the reach of help. I've seen a many people die; little babes and great strong men; and I know when death's a-coming, well enough. But she's troubled in her mind: and when the fits are not on her – and that's not often, for she is dying very hard – she says she has got something to tell, which you must hear. She'll never die quiet till you come, mistress."

At this intelligence, the worthy Mrs Corney muttered a variety of invectives against old women who couldn't even die without purposely annoying their betters; and, muffling herself in a thick shawl which she hastily caught up, briefly requested Mr Bumble to stay till she came back, lest anything particular should occur. Bidding the messenger walk fast, and not be all night hobbling up the stairs, she followed her from the room with a very ill grace, scolding all the way.

Mr Bumble's conduct on being left to himself, was rather inexplicable. He opened the closet, counted the teaspoons, weighed the sugar-tongs, closely inspected a silver milk-pot to ascertain that it was of the genuine metal, and, having satisfied his curiosity on these points, put on his cocked hat corner-wise, and danced with much gravity four distinct times round the table. Having gone through this very extraordinary performance, he took off the cocked hat again, and, spreading himself before the fire with his back towards it, seemed to be mentally engaged in taking an exact inventory of the furniture.

CHAPTER 21

TREATS OF A VERY POOR SUBJECT. BUT IS A SHORT ONE, AND MAY BE FOUND OF IMPORTANCE IN THIS HISTORY

It was no unfit messenger of death, who had disturbed the quiet of the matron's room. Her body was bent by age; her limbs trembled with palsy; her face, distorted into a mumbling leer, resembled more the grotesque shaping of some wild pencil, than the work of Nature's hand.

The old crone tottered along the passages, and up the stairs, muttering some indistinct answers to the chidings of her companion; being at length compelled to pause for breath, she gave the light into her hand, and remained behind to follow as she might: while the more nimble superior made her way to the room where the sick woman lay.

It was a bare garret-room, with a dim light burning at the farther end. There was another old woman watching by the bed; the parish apothecary's apprentice was standing by the fire, making a toothpick out of a quill.

"Cold night, Mrs Corney," said this young gentleman, as the matron entered.

"Very cold, indeed, sir," replied the mistress, in her most civil tones, and dropping a curtsey as she spoke.

"You should get better coals out of your contractors," said the apothecary's deputy, breaking a lump on the top of the fire with the rusty poker; "these are not at all the sort of thing for a cold night."

"They're the board's choosing, sir," returned the matron. "The least they could do, would be to keep us pretty warm: for our places are hard enough."

The conversation was here interrupted by a moan from the sick woman.

"Oh!" said the young man, turning his face towards the bed, as if he had previously quite forgotten the patient, "it's all U.P. there, Mrs Corney."

"It is, is it, sir?" asked the matron.

"If she lasts a couple of hours, I shall be surprised," said the apothecary's apprentice, intent upon the toothpick's point. "It's a break-up of the system altogether. Is she dozing, old lady?"

The attendant stooped over the bed, to ascertain; and nodded in the affirmative.

The apothecary's apprentice, having completed the manufacture of the toothpick, planted himself in front of the fire and made good use of it for ten minutes or so: when apparently growing rather dull, he wished Mrs Corney joy of her job, and took himself off on tiptoe.

When they had sat in silence for some time, the two old women rose from the bed, and crouching over the fire, held out their withered hands to catch the heat. The flame threw a ghastly light on their shrivelled faces, and made their ugliness appear terrible, as, in this position they began to converse in a low voice.

"Did she say any more, Anny dear, while I was gone?" inquired the messenger.

"Not a word," replied the other. "She plucked and tore at her arms for a little time; but I held her hands, and she soon dropped off. She hasn't much strength in her, so I easily kept her quiet. I ain't so weak for an old woman, although I am on parish allowance; no, no!"

"Did she drink the hot wine the doctor said she was to have?" demanded the first.

"I tried to get it down," rejoined the other. "But her teeth were tight set, and she clenched the mug so hard that it was as much as I could do to get it back again. So *I* drank it; and it did me good!"

Looking cautiously round, to ascertain that they were not overheard, the two hags cowered nearer to the fire, and chuckled heartily.

"I mind the time," said the first speaker, "when she would have done the same, and made rare fun of it afterwards."

"Ay, that she would," rejoined the other; "she had a merry heart. A many, many, beautiful corpses she laid out, as nice and neat as waxwork. My old eyes have seen them – ay, and those old hands touched them too; for I have helped her, scores of times."

Stretching forth her trembling fingers as she spoke, the old creature shook them exultingly before her face, and fumbling in her pocket, brought out an old time-discoloured tin snuff-box, from which she shook a few grains into the outstretched palm of her companion, and a few more into her own. While they were thus employed, the matron, who had been impatiently watching until the dying woman should awaken from her stupor, joined them by the fire, and sharply asked how long she was to wait?

"Not long, mistress," replied the second woman, looking up into her face. "We have none of us long to wait for Death. Patience, patience! He'll be here soon enough for us all."

"Hold your tongue, you doting idiot!" said the matron sternly. "You, Martha, tell me; has she been in this way before?"

"Often," answered the first woman.

"But will never be again," added the second one; "that is, she'll never wake again but once – and mind, mistress, that won't be for long!"

"Long or short," said the matron, snappishly, "she won't find me here when she does wake; take care, both of you, how you worry me again for nothing. It's no part of my duty to see all the old women in the house die, and I won't – that's more. Mind that, you impudent old harridans. If you make a fool of me again, I'll soon cure you, I warrant you!"

She was bouncing away, when a cry from the two women, who had turned towards the bed, caused her to look round. The patient had raised herself upright, and was stretching her arms towards them.

"Who's that?" she cried, in a hollow voice.

"Hush, hush!" said one of the women, stooping over her. "Lie down, lie down!"

"I'll never lie down again alive!" said the woman, struggling. "I *will* tell her! Come here! Nearer! Let me whisper in your ear."

She clutched the matron by the arm, and forcing her into a chair by the bedside, was about to speak, when looking round, she caught sight of the two old women bending forward in the attitude of eager listeners.

"Turn them away," said the woman, drowsily; "make haste! make haste!"

The two old crones, chiming in together, began pouring out many piteous lamentations that the poor dear was too far gone to know her best friends; and were uttering sundry protestations that they would never leave her, when the superior pushed them from the room, closed the door, and returned to the bedside. On being excluded, the old ladies changed their tone, and cried through the keyhole that old Sally was drunk; which, indeed, was not unlikely; since, in addition to a moderate dose of opium prescribed by the apothecary, she was labouring under the effects of a final taste of gin-and-water which had been privily administered, in the openness of their hearts, by the worthy old ladies themselves.

"Now listen to me," said the dying woman aloud, as if making a great

effort to revive one latent spark of energy. "In this very room – in this very bed – I once nursed a pretty young creetur', that was brought into the house with her feet cut and bruised with walking, and all soiled with dust and blood. She gave birth to a boy, and died. Let me think – what was the year again?"

"Never mind the year," said the impatient auditor; "what about her?"

"Ay," murmured the sick woman, relapsing into her former drowsy state, "what about her? – what about – I know!" she cried, jumping fiercely up: her face flushed, and her eyes starting from her head – "I robbed her, so I did! She wasn't cold – I tell you she wasn't cold, when I stole it!"

"Stole what, for God's sake?" cried the matron, with a gesture as if she would call for help.

"*It!*" replied the woman, laying her hand over the other's mouth. "The only thing she had. She wanted clothes to keep her warm, and food to eat; but she had kept it safe, and had it in her bosom. It was gold, I tell you! Rich gold, that might have saved her life!"

"Gold!" echoed the matron, bending eagerly over the woman as she fell back. "Go on, go on – yes – what of it? Who was the mother? When was it?"

"She charged me to keep it safe," replied the woman with a groan, "and trusted me as the only woman about her. I stole it in my heart when she first showed it me hanging round her neck; and the child's death, perhaps, is on me besides! They would have treated him better, if they had known it all!"

"Known what?" asked the other. "Speak!"

"The boy grew so like his mother," said the woman, rambling on, and not heeding the question, "that I could never forget it when I saw his face. Poor girl! poor girl! She was so young, too! Such a gentle lamb! Wait;

there's more to tell. I have not told you all, have I?"

"No, no," replied the matron, inclining her head to catch the words, as they came more faintly from the dying woman. "Be quick, or it may be too late!"

"The mother," said the woman, making a more violent effort than before; "the mother, when the pains of death first came upon her, whispered in my ear that if her baby was born alive, and thrived, the day might come when it would not feel so much disgraced to hear its poor young mother named. "And oh, kind Heaven!" she said, folding her thin hands together, "whether it be boy or girl, raise up some friends for it in this troubled world, and take pity upon a lonely desolate child, abandoned to its mercy!"

"The boy's name?" demanded the matron.

"They *called* him Oliver," replied the woman, feebly. "The gold I stole was—"

"Yes, yes – what?" cried the other.

She was bending eagerly over the woman to hear her reply; but drew back, instinctively, as she once again rose, slowly and stiffly, into a sitting posture; then, clutching the coverlid with both hands, muttered some indistinct sounds in her throat, and fell lifeless on the bed.

"Stone dead!" said one of the old women, hurrying in as soon as the door was opened.

"And nothing to tell, after all," rejoined the matron, walking carelessly away.

The two crones, to all appearance, too busily occupied in the preparations for their dreadful duties to make any reply, were left alone, hovering about the body.

CHAPTER 22

WHEREIN THIS HISTORY REVERTS TO MR FAGIN AND COMPANY

While these things were passing in the country workhouse, Mr Fagin sat in the old den – the same from which Oliver had been removed by the girl – brooding over a dull, smoky fire. He held a pair of bellows upon his knee, with which he had apparently been endeavouring to rouse it into more cheerful action; but he had fallen into deep thought; and with his arms folded on them, and his chin resting on his thumbs, fixed his eyes, abstractedly, on the rusty bars.

At a table behind him sat the Artful Dodger, Master Charles Bates, and Mr Chitling: all intent upon a game of whist; the Artful taking dummy against Master Bates and Mr Chitling.

"Hark!" cried the Dodger at this moment, "I heard the tinkler." Catching up the light, he crept softly upstairs.

The bell was rung again, with some impatience, while the party were in darkness. After a short pause, the Dodger reappeared, and whispered to Fagin mysteriously.

"What!" cried the old man, "alone?"

The Dodger nodded in the affirmative, and, shading the flame of the candle with his hand, gave Charley Bates a private intimation, in dumb show, that he had better not be funny just then. Having performed this friendly office, he fixed his eyes on Fagin's face, and awaited his directions.

The old man bit his yellow fingers, and meditated for some seconds; his face working with agitation the while, as if he dreaded something, and feared to know the worst. At length he raised his head.

"Where is he?" he asked.

The Dodger pointed to the floor above, and made a gesture, as if to leave the room.

"Yes," said the old man, answering the mute inquiry; "bring him down. Hush! Quiet, Charley! Gently, Tom! Scarce, scarce!"

This brief direction to Charley Bates, and his recent antagonist, was softly and immediately obeyed. There was no sound of their whereabout, when the Dodger descended the stairs, bearing the light in his hand, and followed by a man in a coarse smock-frock; who, after casting a hurried glance round the room, pulled off a large wrapper which had concealed the lower portion of his face, and disclosed: all haggard, unwashed, and unshorn: the features of flash Toby Crackit.

"How are you, Faguey?" said this worthy, nodding to the old man. "Pop that shawl away in my castor, Dodger, so I may know where to find it when I cut; that's the time of day! You'll be a fine young cracksman afore the old file now."

With these words he pulled up the smock-frock;

and, winding it round his middle, drew a chair to the fire, and placed his feet upon the hob.

"See there, Faguey," he said, pointing disconsolately to his top-boots; "not a drop of Day and Martin since you know when; not a bubble of blacking, by Jove! But don't look at me in that way, man. All in good time. I can't talk about business till I've eat and drank; so produce the sustainance, and let's have a quiet fill-out for the first time these three days!"

The old man motioned to the Dodger to place what eatables there were, upon the table; and, seating himself opposite the housebreaker, waited his leisure.

To judge from appearances, Toby was by no means in a hurry to open the conversation. At first, Fagin contented himself with patiently watching his countenance, as if to gain from its expression some clue to the intelligence he brought; but in vain. He looked tired and worn, but there was the same complacent repose upon his features that they always wore: and through dirt, and beard, and whisker, there still shone, unimpaired, the self-satisfied smirk of flash Toby Crackit. Then, the old man, in an agony of impatience, watched every morsel he put into his mouth; pacing up and down the room, meanwhile, in irrepressible excitement. It was all of no use. Toby continued to eat with the utmost outward indifference, until he could eat no more; then, ordering the Dodger out, he closed the door, mixed a glass of spirits and water, and composed himself for talking.

"First and foremost, Faguey," said Toby.

"Yes, yes," interposed the old man, drawing up his chair.

Mr Crackit stopped to take a draught of spirits and water, and to declare that the gin was excellent; then placing his feet against the low mantelpiece, so as to bring his boots to about the level of his eye, he quietly resumed.

"First and foremost, Faguey," said the housebreaker, "how's Bill?"

"What!" screamed the old man, starting from his seat.

"Why, you don't mean to say—" began Toby, turning pale.

"Mean?" cried the old man, stamping furiously on the ground. "Where are they? Sikes and the boy! Where are they? Where have they been? Where are they hiding? Why have they not been here?"

"The crack failed," said Toby, faintly.

"I know it," replied the old man, tearing a newspaper from his pocket and pointing to it. "What more?"

"They fired and hit the boy. We cut over the fields at the back, with him between us – straight as the crow flies – through hedge and ditch. They gave chase. Damme! the whole country was awake, and the dogs upon us."

"The boy!"

"Bill had him on his back, and scudded like the wind. We stopped to take him between us; his head hung down, and he was cold. They were close upon our heels; every man for himself, and each from the gallows! We parted company, and left the youngster lying in a ditch. Alive or dead, that's all I know about him."

Fagin stopped to hear no more; but uttering a loud yell, and twining his hands in his hair, rushed from the room, and from the house.

CHAPTER 23

IN WHICH A MYSTERIOUS CHARACTER APPEARS UPON THE SCENE; AND MANY THINGS, INSEPARABLE FROM THIS HISTORY, ARE DONE AND PERFORMED

Near to the top on which Snow Hill and Holborn Hill meet, there opens, upon the right hand as you come out of the City, a narrow and dismal alley leading to Saffron Hill. In its filthy shops are exposed for sale huge bunches of second-hand silk handkerchiefs, of all sizes and patterns; for here reside the traders who purchase them from pick-pockets.

It was into this place that Fagin turned. He was well known to the sallow denizens of the lane; for such of them as were on the look-out to buy or sell, nodded, familiarly, as he passed along. He replied to their salutations in the same way; but bestowed no closer recognition until he reached the further end of the alley; when he stopped, to address a salesman of small stature. Pointing in the direction of Saffron Hill, he inquired whether any one was up yonder tonight.

"At the Cripples?" inquired the man.

Fagin nodded.

"Yes, there's some half-dozen of 'em gone in. I don't mind if I have a drop there with you!"

But the old man, looking back, waved his hand to intimate that he preferred being alone.

Fagin walked straight upstairs, and opening the door of a room, and softly insinuating himself into the chamber, looked anxiously about: shading his eyes with his hand, as if in search of some particular person.

The room was illuminated by two gas-lights; the glare of which was prevented by the barred shutters, and closely-drawn curtains of faded red, from being visible outside. The ceiling was blackened, to prevent its colour from being injured by the flaring of the lamps; and the place was so full of dense tobacco smoke, that at first it was scarcely possible to discern anything more. By degrees, however, as some of it cleared away through the open door, an assemblage of heads, as confused as the noises that greeted the ear, might be made out; and as the eye grew more accustomed to the scene, the spectator gradually became aware of the presence of a numerous company, male and female, crowded round a long table: at the upper end of which, sat a chairman with a hammer of office in his hand; while a professional gentleman, with a bluish nose, and his face tied up for the benefit of a toothache, presided at a jingling piano in a remote corner.

Fagin looked eagerly from face to face; apparently without meeting that of which he was in search. Succeeding, at length, in catching the eye of the man who occupied the chair, he beckoned to him slightly, and left the room, as quietly as he had entered it.

"What can I do for you, Mr Fagin?" inquired the man, as he followed him out to the landing. "Won't you join us? They'll be delighted, every one of 'em."

Fagin shook his head impatiently, and said in a whisper, "Is *he* here?"

"No," replied the man.

"And no news of Barney?" inquired Fagin.

"None," replied the landlord of the Cripples; for it was he. "He won't

stir till it's all safe. Depend on it, they're on the scent down there; and that if he moved, he'd blow upon the thing at once. He's all right enough, Barney is, else I should have heard of him. I'll pound it, that Barney's managing properly. Let him alone for that."

"Will *he* be here tonight?" asked the old man.

"Monks, do you mean?" inquired the landlord, hesitating.

"Hush!" said the old man. "Yes."

"Certain," replied the man, drawing a gold watch from his fob; "I expected him here before now. If you'll wait ten minutes, he'll be—"

"No, no," said the old man, hastily; as though, however desirous he might be to see the person in question, he was nevertheless relieved by his absence. "Tell him I came here to see him; and that he must come to me tonight. No, say tomorrow. As he is not here, tomorrow will be time enough."

"Good!" said the man. "Nothing more?"

"Not a word now," said the old man, descending the stairs.

Fagin was no sooner alone, than his countenance resumed its former expression of anxiety and thought. After a brief reflection, he called a hack cabriolet, and bade the man drive towards Bethnal Green. He dismissed him within some quarter of a mile of Mr Sikes's residence, and performed the short remainder of the distance on foot.

"Now," muttered the old man, as he knocked at the door, "if there is any deep play here, I shall have it out of you, my girl, cunning as you are."

She was in her room, the woman said. Fagin crept softly upstairs, and entered it without any previous ceremony. The girl was alone: lying with her head upon the table, and her hair straggling over it.

"She has been drinking," thought the old man, coolly, "or perhaps she is only miserable."

During the silence, the old man looked restlessly about the room, as if

to assure himself that there were no appearances of Sikes having covertly returned. Apparently satisfied with his inspection, he coughed twice or thrice, and made as many efforts to open a conversation; but the girl heeded him no more than if he had been made of stone. At length he made another attempt; and rubbing his hands together, said, in his most conciliatory tone,

"And where should you think Bill was now, my dear?"

The girl moaned out some half intelligible reply, that she could not tell; and seemed, from the smothered noise that escaped her, to be crying.

"And the boy, too," said Fagin, straining his eyes to catch a glimpse of her face. "Poor leetle child! Left in a ditch, Nance; only think!"

"The child," said the girl, suddenly looking up, "is better where he is, than among us; and if no harm comes to Bill from it, I hope he lies dead in the ditch, and that his young bones may rot there."

"Listen to me, you drab. Listen to me, who, with six words, can strangle Sikes as surely as if I had his bull's throat between my fingers now. If he comes back, and leaves the boy behind him – if he gets off free, and, dead or alive, fails to restore him to me; murder him yourself if you would have him escape Jack Ketch. And do it the moment he sets foot in this room, or mind me, it will be too late!"

"What is all this?" cried the girl involuntarily.

"What is it?" pursued Fagin, mad with rage. "When the boy's worth hundreds of pounds to me, am I to lose what chance threw me in the way of getting safely, through the whims of a drunken gang that I could whistle away the lives of! And me bound, too, to a born devil that only wants the will, and has the power to, to—"

"Don't worry me now, Fagin!" replied the girl, raising her head languidly. "If Bill has not done it this time, he will another. He has done many a good job for you, and will do many more when he can; and when he can't he won't; so no more about that."

"Regarding this boy, my dear?" said the old man, rubbing the palms of his hands nervously together.

"The boy must take his chance with the rest," interrupted Nancy, hastily; "and I say again, I hope he is dead, and out of harm's way, and out of yours – that is, if Bill comes to no harm. And if Toby got clear off, Bill's pretty sure to be safe; for Bill's worth two of Toby any time."

"And about what I was saying, my dear?" observed the old man, keeping his glistening eye steadily upon her.

"You must say it all over again, if it's anything you want me to do," rejoined Nancy; "and if it is, you had better wait till tomorrow. You put me up for a minute; but now I'm stupid again."

Having eased his mind by this discovery; and having accomplished his twofold object of imparting to the girl what he had, that night, heard, and of ascertaining, with his own eyes, that Sikes had not returned, Mr Fagin again turned his face homeward: leaving his young friend asleep, with her head upon the table.

It was within an hour of midnight. The weather being dark, and piercing cold, he had no great temptation to loiter. The sharp wind that scoured the streets, seemed to have cleared them of passengers, as of dust and mud, for few people were abroad, and they were to all appearance hastening fast home. It blew from the right quarter for the old man, however, and straight before it he went: trembling, and shivering, as every fresh gust drove him rudely on his way.

He had reached the corner of his own street, and was already fumbling in his pocket for the door-key, when a dark figure emerged from a projecting entrance which lay in deep shadow, and, crossing the road, glided up to him unperceived.

"Fagin!" whispered a voice close to his ear.

"Ah!" said the old man, turning quickly round, "is that—"

"Yes!" interrupted the stranger. "I have been lingering here these two hours. Where the devil have you been?"

"On your business, my dear," replied the old man, glancing uneasily at his companion, and slackening his pace as he spoke. "On your business all night."

"Oh, of course!" said the stranger, with a sneer. "Well; and what's come of it?"

"Nothing good," said the old man.

"Nothing bad, I hope?" said the stranger, stopping short, and turning a startled look on his companion.

The old man shook his head, and was about to reply, when the stranger, interrupting him, motioned to the house, before which they had by this time arrived: remarking, that he had better say what he had got to say, under cover: for his blood was chilled with standing about so long, and the wind blew through him.

Fagin looked as if he could have willingly excused himself from taking home a visitor at that unseasonable hour; and, indeed, muttered something about having no fire; but his companion repeating his request in a peremptory manner, he unlocked the door, and requested him to close it softly, while he got a light.

"It's as dark as the grave," said the man, groping forward a few steps.

"Make haste!"

"Shut the door," whispered Fagin from the end of the passage. As he spoke, it closed with a loud noise.

"That wasn't my doing," said the other man, feeling his way. "The wind blew it to, or it shut of its own accord: one or the other. Look sharp with the light, or I shall knock my brains out against something in this confounded hole."

Fagin stealthily descended the kitchen stairs. After a short absence, he returned with a lighted candle, and the intelligence that Toby Crackit was asleep in the back room below, and that the boys were in the front one. Beckoning the man to follow him, he led the way upstairs.

"We can say the few words we've got to say in here, my dear," said the old man, throwing open a door on the first floor; "and as there are holes in the shutters, and we never show lights to our neighbours, we'll set the candle on the stairs. There!"

They conversed for some time in whispers. They might have been talking, thus, for a quarter of an hour or more, when Monks – by which name Fagin had designated the strange man several times in the course of their colloquy – said, raising his voice a little,

"I tell you again, it was badly planned. Why not have kept him here among the rest, and made a sneaking, snivelling pickpocket of him at once?"

"Only hear him!" exclaimed the old man, shrugging his shoulders.

"Why, do you mean to say you couldn't have done it, if you had chosen?" demanded Monks, sternly. "Haven't you done it, with other boys, scores of times? If you had had patience for a twelvemonth, at most, couldn't you have got him convicted, and sent safely out of the kingdom; perhaps for life?"

"Whose turn would that have served, my dear?" inquired the old man humbly.

"Mine," replied Monks.

"But not mine," said the old man, submissively. "He might have become of use to me. When there are two parties to a bargain, it is only reasonable that the interests of both should be consulted; is it, my good friend?"

"What then?" demanded Monks.

"I saw it was not easy to train him to the business," replied Fagin; "he was not like other boys in the same circumstances."

"Curse him, no!" muttered the man, "or he would have been a thief, long ago."

"I had no hold upon him to make him worse," pursued the old man, anxiously watching the countenance of his companion. "His hand was not in. I had nothing to frighten him with; which we always must have in the beginning, or we labour in vain. What could I do? Send him out with the Dodger and Charley? We had enough of that, at first, my dear; I trembled for us all."

"*That* was not my doing," observed Monks.

"No, no, my dear!" renewed the old man. "And I don't quarrel with it now; because, if it had never happened, you might never have clapped eyes upon the boy to notice him, and so led to the discovery that it was him you were looking for. Well! I got him back for you by means of the girl; and then *she* begins to favour him."

"Throttle the girl!" said Monks, impatiently.

"Why, we can't afford to do that just now, my dear," replied the old man, smiling; "and, besides, that sort of thing is not in our way; or, one of these days, I might be glad to have it done. I know what these girls are, Monks, well. As soon as the boy begins to harden, she'll care no more for him, than for a block of wood. You want him made a thief. If he is alive, I can make him one from this time; and, if – if – " said the old man, drawing nearer to the other, – "it's not likely, mind – but if the worst comes to the worst, and he is dead—"

"It's no fault of mine if he is!" interposed the other man, with a look of terror, and clasping the old man's arm with trembling hands. "Mind that, Fagin! I had no hand in it. Anything but his death, I told you from the first. I won't shed blood; it's always found out, and haunts a man besides. If they shot him dead, I was not the cause; do you hear me? Fire this infernal den— What's that?"

"What!" cried the old man, grasping the coward round the body, with both arms, as he sprung to his feet. "Where?"

"Yonder!" replied the man, glaring at the opposite wall. "The shadow! I saw the shadow of a woman, in a cloak and bonnet, pass along the wainscot like a breath!"

The old man released his hold, and they rushed tumultuously from the room. The candle, wasted by the draught, was standing where it had been placed. It showed them only the empty staircase, and their own white faces. They listened intently: a profound silence reigned throughout the house.

"It's your fancy," said the old man, taking up the light and turning to his companion.

"I'll swear I saw it!" replied Monks, trembling. "It was bending forward when I saw it first; and when I spoke, it darted away."

The old man glanced contemptuously at the pale face of his associate, and, telling him he could follow, if he pleased, ascended the stairs. They looked into all the rooms; they were cold, bare, and empty. They descended into the passage, and thence into the cellars below. The green damp hung upon the low walls; the tracks of the snail and slug glistened in the light of the candle; but all was still as death.

"What do you think now?" said Fagin, when they had regained the passage. "Besides ourselves, there's not a creature in the house except Toby and the boys; and they're safe enough. See here!"

As a proof of the fact, the old man drew forth two keys from his pocket; and explained that when he first went downstairs, he had locked them in, to prevent any intrusion on the conference.

This accumulated testimony effectually staggered Mr Monks. His protestations had gradually become less and less vehement as they proceeded in their search without making any discovery; and, now, he gave vent to several very grim laughs, and confessed it could only have been his excited imagination. He declined any renewal of the conversation, however, for that night: suddenly remembering that it was past one o'clock. And so the amiable couple parted.

CHAPTER 24

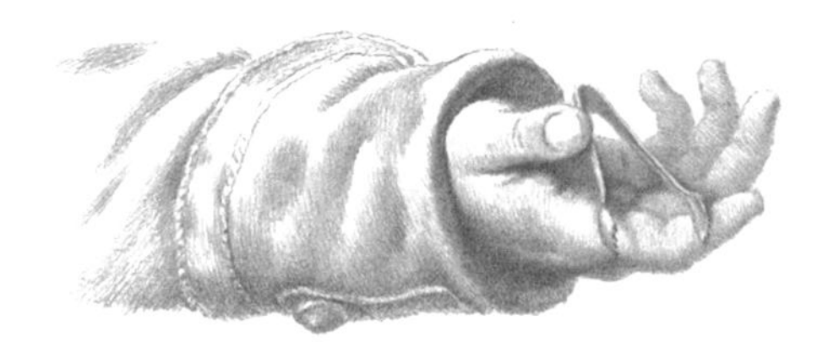

ATONES FOR THE UNPOLITENESS OF A FORMER CHAPTER; WHICH DESERTED A LADY, MOST UNCEREMONIOUSLY

Mr Bumble had re-counted the teaspoons, re-weighed the sugar-tongs, made a closer inspection of the milk-pot, and ascertained to a nicety the exact condition of the furniture, down to the very horse-hair seats of the chairs; and had repeated each process full half a dozen times; before he began to think that it was time for Mrs Corney to return. Thinking begets thinking; as there were no sounds of Mrs Corney's approach, it occurred to Mr Bumble that it would be an innocent and virtuous way of spending the time, if he were further to allay his curiousity by a cursory glance at the interior of Mrs Corney's chest of drawers.

He was still placidly engaged in this latter survey, when Mrs Corney, hurrying into the room, threw herself, in a breathless state, on a chair by the fireside, and covering her eyes with one hand, placed the other over her heart, and gasped for breath.

"Mrs Corney," said Mr Bumble, stooping over the matron, "what is this, ma'am? Has anything happened, ma'am? Pray answer me; I'm on – on –" Mr Bumble, in his alarm, could not immediately think of the word "tenter-hooks," so he said "broken bottles."

"Oh, Mr Bumble!" cried the lady, "I have been so dreadfully put out!"

"Put out, ma'am!" exclaimed Mr Bumble; "who has dared to—? I know!" said Mr Bumble, checking himself, with native majesty, "this is them wicious paupers!"

"It's dreadful to think of!" said the lady, shuddering.

"Then *don't* think of it, ma'am," rejoined Mr Bumble.

"I can't help it," whimpered the lady.

"Don't sigh, Mrs Corney," said Mr Bumble.

"I can't help it," said Mrs Corney. And she sighed again.

"This is a very comfortable room, ma'am," said Mr Bumble, looking round. "Another room, and this, ma'am, would be a complete thing."

"It would be too much for one," murmured the lady.

"But not for two, ma'am," rejoined Mr Bumble, in soft accents. "Eh, Mrs Corney?"

Mrs Corney drooped her head, when the beadle said this; the beadle drooped his, to get a view of Mrs Corney's face. Mrs Corney, with great propriety, turned her head away, and released her hand to get at her pocket-handkerchief; but insensibly replaced it in that of Mr Bumble.

"The board allows you coals, don't they, Mrs Corney?" inquired the beadle, affectionately pressing her hand.

"And candles," replied Mrs Corney, slightly returning the pressure.

"Coals, candles, and house-rent free," said Mr Bumble. "Oh, Mrs Corney, what an Angel you are!"

The lady was not proof against this burst of feeling. She sank into Mr Bumble's arms; and that gentleman, in his agitation, imprinted a passionate kiss upon her chaste nose.

"Such porochial perfection!" exclaimed Mr Bumble rapturously. "You know that Mr Slout is worse tonight, my fascinator?"

"Yes," replied Mrs Corney, bashfully.

"He can't live a week, the doctor says," pursued Mr Bumble. "He is the master of this establishment; his death will cause a wacancy: that wacancy must be filled up. Oh, Mrs Corney, what a prospect this opens! What a opportunity for a jining of hearts and housekeepings!"

Mrs Corney sobbed.

"The little word?" said Mr Bumble, bending over the bashful beauty. "The one little, little, little word, my blessed Corney?"

"Ye – ye – yes!" sighed out the matron.

"One more," pursued the beadle; "compose your darling feelings for only one more. When is it to come off?"

Mrs Corney twice essayed to speak: and twice failed. At length summoning up courage, she threw her arms round Mr Bumble's neck, and said, it might be as soon as ever he pleased, and that he was "a irresistible duck."

Matters being thus amicably and satisfactorily arranged, the contract was solemnly ratified in a teacupful of peppermint mixture; which was rendered the more necessary, by the flutter and agitation of the lady's spirits. While it was being disposed of, she acquainted Mr Bumble with the old woman's decease.

"Very good," said that gentleman, sipping his peppermint; "I'll call at Sowerberry's as I go home, and tell him to send tomorrow morning. Was it that as frightened you, love?"

"It wasn't anything particular, dear," said the lady, evasively.

"It must have been something, love," urged Mr Bumble. "Won't you tell your own B.?"

"Not now," rejoined the lady; "one of these days. After we're married, dear."

"After we're married!" exclaimed Mr Bumble. "It wasn't any impudence from any of them male paupers as—"

"No, no, love!" interposed the lady, hastily.

"If I thought it was," continued Mr Bumble; "if I thought as any one of 'em had dared to lift his wulgar eyes to that lovely countenance—"

"They wouldn't have dared to do it, love," responded the lady.

"They had better not!" said Mr Bumble, clenching his fist. "Let me see any man, porochial or extra-porochial, as would presume to do it; and I can tell him that he wouldn't do it a second time!"

Unembellished by any violence of gesticulation, this might have seemed no very high compliment to the lady's charms; but, as Mr Bumble accompanied the threat with many warlike gestures, she was much touched with this proof of his devotion, and protested, with great admiration, that he was indeed a dove.

The dove then turned up his coat-collar, and put on his cocked hat; and, having exchanged a long and affectionate embrace with his future partner, once again braved the cold wind of the night: merely pausing, for a few minutes, in the male paupers' ward, to abuse them a little, with the view of satisfying himself that he could fill the office of workhouse-master with needful acerbity. Assured of his qualifications, Mr Bumble left the building with a light heart, and bright visions of his future promotion: which served to occupy his mind until he reached the shop of the undertaker.

CHAPTER 25

LOOKS AFTER OLIVER, AND PROCEEDS WITH HIS ADVENTURES

"Wolves tear your throats!" muttered Sikes, grinding his teeth. "I wish I was among some of you; you'd howl the hoarser for it."

As Sikes growled forth this imprecation, with the most desperate ferocity that his desperate nature was capable of, he rested the body of the wounded boy across his bended knee; and turned his head, for an instant, to look back at his pursuers.

There was little to be made out, in the mist and darkness; but the loud shouting of men vibrated through the air, and the barking of the neighbouring dogs, roused by the sound of the alarm bell, resounded in every direction.

"Stop, you white-livered hound!" cried the robber, shouting after Toby Crackit, who, making the best use of his long legs, was already ahead. "Stop!"

The repetition of the word, brought Toby to a dead standstill. For he was not quite satisfied that he was beyond the range of pistol-shot; and Sikes was in no mood to be played with.

"Bear a hand with the boy," cried Sikes, beckoning furiously to his confederate. "Come back!"

Toby made a show of returning; but ventured, in a low voice, broken for want of breath, to intimate considerable reluctance as he came slowly along.

"Quicker!" cried Sikes, laying the boy in a dry ditch at his feet, and drawing a pistol from his pocket. "Don't play booty with me."

At this moment the noise grew louder. Sikes, again looking round, could discern that the men who had given chase were already climbing the gate of the field in which he stood; and that a couple of dogs were some paces in advance of them.

"It's all up, Bill!" cried Toby; "drop the kid, and show 'em your heels." With this parting advice, Mr Crackit, preferring the chance of being shot by his friend, to the certainty of being taken by his enemies, fairly turned tail, and darted off at full speed. Sikes clenched his teeth; took one look around; threw over the prostrate form of Oliver the cape in which he had been hurriedly muffled; ran along the front of the hedge, as if to distract the attention of those behind, from the spot where the boy lay; paused, for a second, before another hedge which met it at right angles; and whirling his pistol high into the air, cleared it at a bound, and was gone.

At length, a low cry of pain broke the stillness that prevailed; and uttering it, the boy awoke. His left arm, rudely bandaged in a shawl, hung heavy and useless at his side: the bandage was saturated with blood. He was so weak, that he could scarcely raise himself into a sitting posture; when he had done so, he looked feebly round for help, and groaned with pain. Trembling in every joint, from cold and exhaustion, he made an effort to stand upright; but, shuddering from head to foot, fell prostrate on the ground.

After a short return of the stupor in which he had been so long plunged, Oliver: urged by a creeping sickness at his heart, which seemed to warn him that if he lay there, he must surely die: got upon his feet, and essayed to walk. His head was dizzy, and he staggered to and fro like a drunken man. But he kept up, nevertheless, and, with his head drooping languidly on his breast, went stumbling onward, he knew not whither.

Thus he staggered on, creeping, almost mechanically, between the bars of gates, or through hedge-gaps as they came in his way, until he reached a road. Here the rain began to fall so heavily, that it roused him.

He looked about, and saw that at no great distance there was a house, which perhaps he could reach. Pitying his condition, they might have compassion on him; and if they did not, it would be better, he thought, to die near human beings, than in the lonely open fields. He summoned up all his strength for one last trial, and bent his faltering steps towards it.

As he drew nearer to this house, a feeling came over him that he had seen it before. He remembered nothing of its details; but the shape and aspect of the building seemed familiar to him.

That garden wall! On the grass inside he had fallen on his knees last night, and prayed the two men's mercy. It was the very house they had attempted to rob.

Oliver felt such fear come over him when he recognized the place, that, for the instant, he forgot the agony of his wound, and thought only of flight. Flight! He could scarcely stand: and if he were in full possession of all the best powers of his slight and youthful frame, whither could he fly? He pushed against the garden-gate; it was unlocked, and swung open on its hinges. He tottered across the lawn; climbed the steps; knocked faintly at the door; and, his whole strength failing him, sunk down against one of the pillars of the little portico.

It happened that about this time, Mr Giles, Brittles, and the tinker, were recruiting themselves, after the fatigues and terrors of the night, with tea and sundries, in the kitchen.

The cook and housemaid screamed.

"It was a knock," said Mr Giles, assuming perfect serenity. "Open the door, somebody."

Nobody moved.

"It seems a strange sort of a thing, a knock coming at such a time in the morning," said Mr Giles, surveying the pale faces which surrounded him, and looking very blank himself; "but the door must be opened. Do you hear, somebody?"

Brittles, who had got behind the door to open it, no sooner saw Oliver, than he uttered a loud cry. Mr Giles, seizing the boy by one leg and one arm (fortunately not the broken limb) lugged him straight into the hall, and deposited him at full length on the floor thereof.

"Here he is!" bawled Giles, calling, in a state of great excitement, up the staircase; "here's one of the thieves, ma'am! Here's a thief, miss! Wounded, miss! I shot him, miss; and Brittles held the light."

" – In a lantern, miss," cried Brittles, applying one hand to the side of his mouth, so that his voice might travel the better.

The two women-servants ran upstairs to carry the intelligence that Mr Giles had captured a robber; and the tinker busied himself in endeavouring to restore Oliver, lest he should die before he could be hanged. In the midst of all this noise and commotion, there was heard a sweet female voice, which quelled it in an instant.

"Giles!" whispered the voice from the stair-head.

"I'm here, miss," replied Mr Giles. "Don't be frightened, miss; I ain't much injured. He didn't make a very desperate resistance, miss! I was soon too many for him."

"Hush!" replied the young lady; "you frighten my aunt as much as the

thieves did. Is the poor creature much hurt?"

"Wounded desperate, miss," replied Giles, with indescribable complacency.

"He looks as if he was a-going, miss," bawled Brittles, in the same manner as before. "Wouldn't you like to come and look at him, miss, in case he should?"

"Hush, pray; there's a good man!" rejoined the lady. "Wait quietly only one instant, while I speak to aunt."

With a footstep as soft and gentle as the voice, the speaker tripped away. She soon returned, with the direction that the wounded person was to be carried, carefully, upstairs to Mr Giles's room; and that Brittles was to saddle the pony and betake himself instantly to Chertsey: from which place he was to despatch, with all speed, a constable and doctor.

"But won't you take one look at him, first, miss?" asked Mr Giles, with as much pride as if Oliver were some bird of rare plumage, that he had skilfully brought down. "Not one little peep, miss?"

"Not now, for the world," replied the young lady. "Poor fellow! Oh! treat him kindly, Giles for my sake!"

The old servant looked up at the speaker, as she turned away, with a glance as proud and admiring as if she had been his own child. Then, bending over Oliver, he helped to carry him upstairs, with the care and solicitude of a woman.

CHAPTER 26

INVOLVES A CRITICAL POSITION

"Who's that?" inquired Brittles, opening the door a little way, with the chain up, and peeping out, shading the candle with his hand.

"Open the door," replied a man outside; "it's the officers from Bow Street, as was sent to today."

The man who had knocked at the door, was a stout personage of middle height, aged about fifty: with shiny black hair, cropped pretty close; half-whiskers, a round face, and sharp eyes. The other was a red-headed, bony man, in top-boots; with a rather ill-favoured countenance, and a turned-up sinister-looking nose.

"Tell your governor that Blathers and Duff is here, will you?" said the stouter man, smoothing down his hair, and laying a pair of handcuffs on the table. "Oh! Good evening, master. Can I have a word or two with you in private, if you please?"

This was addressed to Mr Losberne, who now made his appearance; that gentleman, motioning Brittles to retire, brought in the two ladies, and shut the door. The reader may be informed, that Mr Losberne, a surgeon in the neighbourhood, known through a circuit of ten miles round as "the doctor", had grown fat, more hearty, and withal as eccentric an old batchelor, as will be found in five times that space, by any explorer alive.

"This is the lady of the house," said Mr Losberne, motioning towards Mrs Maylie.

Mr Blathers made a bow. Being desired to sit down, he put his hat on the floor, and taking a chair, motioned Duff to do the same. The latter gentleman, who did not appear quite so much accustomed to good society, or quite so much at his ease in it – one of the two – seated himself, after undergoing several muscular affections of the limbs, and forced the head of his stick into his mouth, with some embarrassment.

"Now, with regard to this here robbery, master," said Blathers. "What are the circumstances?"

Mr Losberne, who appeared desirous of gaining time, recounted them at great length, and with much circumlocution. Messrs Blathers and Duff looked very knowing meanwhile, and occasionally exchanged a nod.

"I can't say, for certain, till I see the work, of course," said Blathers; "but my opinion at once is – I don't mind committing myself to that extent – that this wasn't done by a yokel; eh, Duff?"

"Certainly not," replied Duff.

"And, translating the word yokel for the benefit of the ladies, I apprehend your meaning to be, that this attempt was not made by a countryman?" said Mr Losberne, with a smile.

"That's it, master," replied Blathers. "This is all about the robbery, is it?"

"All," replied the doctor.

"Now, what is this, about this here boy that the servants are a-talking on?" said Blathers.

"Nothing at all," replied the doctor. "One of the frightened servants chose to take it into his head, that he had something to do with this attempt to break into the house; but it's nonsense: sheer absurdity."

With the next morning, there came a rumour, that two men and a boy were in the cage at Kingston, who had been apprehended overnight under suspicious circumstances; and to Kingston Messrs Blathers and Duff journeyed accordingly. The suspicious circumstances, however, resolving themselves, on investigation, into the one fact, that they had been discovered sleeping under a haystack; which, although a great crime, is only punishable by imprisonment, and is, in the merciful eye of the English law, and its comprehensive love of all the king's subjects, held to be no satisfactory proof, in the absence of all other evidence, that the sleeper, or sleepers, have committed burglary accompanied with violence, and have therefore rendered themselves liable to the punishment of death; Messrs Blathers and Duff came back again, as wise as they went.

In short, after some more examination, and a great deal more conversation, a neighbouring magistrate was readily induced to take the joint bail of Mrs Maylie and Mr Losberne for Oliver's appearance if he should ever be called upon; and Blathers and Duff, being rewarded with a couple of guineas, returned to town with divided opinions on the subject of their expedition.

Meanwhile, Oliver gradually throve and prospered under the united care of Mrs Maylie, Rose, and the kind-hearted Mr Losberne. If fervent prayers, gushing from hearts overcharged with gratitude, be heard in heaven – and if they be not, what prayers are! – the blessings which the orphan child called down upon them, sunk into their souls, diffusing peace and happiness.

CHAPTER 27

OF THE HAPPY LIFE OLIVER BEGAN TO LEAD WITH HIS KIND FRIENDS

Oliver's ailings were neither slight nor few. In addition to the pain and delay attendant on a broken limb, his exposure to the wet and cold had brought on fever and ague: which hung about him for many weeks. But, at length, he began, by slow degrees, to get better, and to be able to say sometimes how deeply he felt the goodness of the two sweet ladies, and how ardently he hoped that when he grew strong and well again, he could do something to show his gratitude; something, however slight, which would prove to them that their gentle kindness had not been cast away; but that the poor boy whom their charity had rescued from misery, or death, was eager to serve them with his whole heart and soul.

"Poor fellow!" said Rose, when Oliver had been one day feebly endeavouring to utter the words of thankfulness that rose to his pale lips: "you shall have many opportunities of serving us, if you will. We are going into the country, and my aunt intends that you shall accompany us. The quiet place, the pure air, and all the pleasures and beauties of spring, will restore you in a few days. We will employ you in a hundred ways, when you can bear the trouble."

"The trouble!" cried Oliver. "Oh! dear lady, if I could but work for you;

if I could only give you pleasure by watering your flowers, or watching your birds, or running up and down the whole day long, to make you happy; what would I give to do it!"

"You shall give nothing at all," said Miss Maylie, smiling; "for, as I told you before, we shall employ you in a hundred ways; and if you only take half the trouble to please us, that you promise now, you will make me very happy indeed."

"Happy, ma'am!" cried Oliver; "how kind of you to say so!"

"You will make me happier than I can tell you," replied the young lady. "To think that my dear good aunt should have been the means of rescuing any one from such sad misery as you have described to us, would be an unspeakable pleasure to me; but to know that the object of her goodness and compassion was sincerely grateful and attached, in consequence, would delight me, more than you can well imagine. Do you understand me?" she inquired, watching Oliver's thoughtful face.

"Oh yes, ma'am, yes!" replied Oliver eagerly; "but I was thinking that I am ungrateful now."

"To whom?" inquired the young lady.

"To the kind gentleman, and the dear old nurse, who took so much care of me before," rejoined Oliver. "If they knew how happy I am, they would be pleased, I am sure."

"I am sure they would," rejoined Oliver's benefactress; "and Mr Losberne has already been kind enough to promise that when you are well enough to bear the journey, he will carry you to see them."

"Has he, ma'am?" cried Oliver, his face brightening with pleasure. "I don't know what I shall do for joy when I see their kind faces once again!"

In a short time Oliver was sufficiently recovered to undergo the fatigue of this expedition. One morning he and Mr Losberne set out, accordingly, in a little carriage which belonged to Mrs Maylie.

As Oliver knew the name of the street in which Mr Brownlow resided, they were enabled to drive straight thither. When the coach turned into it, his heart beat so violently, that he could scarcely draw his breath.

"Now, my boy, which house is it?" inquired Mr Losberne.

"That! That!" replied Oliver, pointing eagerly out of the window. "The white house. Oh! make haste! Pray make haste! I feel as if I should die; it makes me tremble so."

"Come, come!" said the good doctor, patting him on the shoulder. "You will see them directly, and they will be overjoyed to find you safe and well."

"Oh! I hope so!" cried Oliver. "They were so good to me; so very, very good to me."

The coach rolled on. It stopped. No; that was the wrong house; the next door. It went on a few paces, and stopped again. Oliver looked up at the windows, with tears of happy expectation coursing down his face.

Alas! the white house was empty and there was a bill in the window. "To Let."

"Knock at the next door," cried Mr Losberne, taking Oliver's arm in his. "What has become of Mr Brownlow, who used to live in the adjoining house, do you know?"

The servant did not know; but would go and inquire. She presently returned, and said, that Mr Brownlow had sold off his goods, and gone to the West Indies, six weeks before. Oliver clasped his hands, and sank feebly backward.

"Has his housekeeper gone, too?" inquired Mr Losberne.

"Yes, sir;" replied the servant. "The old gentleman, the housekeeper, and a gentleman who was a friend of Mr Brownlow's, all went together."

"Then turn towards home again," said Mr Losberne to the driver; "and don't stop to bait the horses, till you get out of this confounded London!"

"The book-stall keeper, sir?" said Oliver. "I know the way there. See him, pray, sir! Do see him!"

"My poor boy, this is disappointment enough for one day," said the doctor. "Quite enough for both of us. If we go to the book-stall keeper's, we shall certainly find that he is dead, or has set his house on fire, or run away. No; home again straight!" And in obedience to the doctor's impulse, home they went.

This bitter disappointment caused Oliver much sorrow and grief, even in the midst of his happiness; for he had pleased himself, many times during his illness, with thinking of all that Mr Brownlow and Mrs Bedwin would say to him: and what delight it would be to tell them how many long days and nights he had passed in reflecting on what they had done for him, and in bewailing his cruel separation from them. The hope of eventually clearing himself with them had buoyed him up, and sustained him, under many of his recent trials; and now, the idea that they should have gone so far, and carried with them the belief that he was an impostor and a robber was almost more than he could bear.

The circumstance occasioned no alteration, however, in the behaviour of his benefactors. After another fortnight, when the fine warm weather had fairly begun, they departed to a cottage at some distance in the country, and took Oliver with them.

So three months glided away; three months which, in the life of the most blessed and favoured of mortals, might have been unmingled happiness, and which, in Oliver's, were true felicity. With the purest and most amiable generosity on one side; and the truest, warmest, soul-felt gratitude on the other; it is no wonder that, by the end of that short time,

Oliver Twist had become completely domesticated with the old lady and her niece, and that the fervent attachment of his young and sensitive heart, was repaid by their pride in, and attachment to, himself.

CHAPTER 28

IN WHICH MR BUMBLE MAKES THE ACQUAINTANCE OF A MYSTERIOUS PERSONAGE

Mr Bumble walked up one street, and down another, until exercise had abated the first passion of his grief; and then the revulsion of feeling made him thirsty. He passed a great many public-houses; but, at length paused before one in a by-way, whose parlour, as he gathered from a hasty peep over the blinds, was deserted, save by one solitary customer. He eyed Bumble askance, as he entered, but scarcely deigned to nod his head in acknowledgment of his salutation.

Mr Bumble had quite dignity enough for two: supposing even that the stranger had been more familiar: so he drank his gin-and-water in silence, and read the paper with great show of pomp and circumstance.

It so happened, however: as it will happen very often, when men fall into company under such circumstances: that Mr Bumble felt, every now and then, a powerful inducement, which he could not resist, to steal a look at the stranger: and that whenever he did so, he withdrew his eyes, in some confusion, to find that the stranger was at that moment stealing a look at him.

"I have seen you before, I think?" said he. "You were differently dressed at that time, and I only passed you in the street, but I should know you again. You were beadle here, once; were you not?"

"I was," said Mr Bumble, in some surprise; "porochial beadle."

"Just so," rejoined the other, nodding his head. "It was in that character I saw you. What are you now?"

"Master of the workhouse," rejoined Mr Bumble, slowly and impressively, to check any undue familiarity the stranger might otherwise assume. "Master of the workhouse, young man!"

The stranger smiled, and nodded his head again: as much as to say, he had not mistaken his man; then rang the bell.

"Fill this glass again," he said, handing Mr Bumble's empty tumbler to the landlord. "Let it be strong and hot. You like it so, I suppose?"

"Not too strong," replied Mr Bumble, with a delicate cough.

"You understand what that means, landlord!" said the stranger, drily.

The host smiled, disappeared, and shortly afterwards returned with a steaming jorum: of which the first gulp brought the water into Mr Bumble's eyes.

"Now listen to me," said the stranger, after closing the door and window. "I came down to this place today, to find you out; and, by one of those chances which the devil throws in the way of his friends sometimes, you walked into the very room I was sitting in, while you were uppermost in my mind. I want some information from you. I don't ask you to give it for nothing, slight as it is. Put up that, to begin with."

As he spoke, he pushed a couple of sovereigns across the table to his companion, carefully, as though unwilling that the chinking of money should be heard without. When Mr Bumble had scrupulously examined the coins, to see that they were genuine, and had put them up, with much satisfaction, in his waistcoat-pocket, he went on:

"Carry your memory back – let me see – twelve years, last winter."

"It's a long time," said Mr Bumble. "Very good. I've done it."

"The scene, the workhouse."

"Good!"

"And the time, night."

"Yes."

"And the place, the crazy hole, wherever it was, in which miserable drabs brought forth the life and health so often denied to themselves – gave birth to puling children for the parish to rear; and hid their shame, rot 'em in the grave!"

"The lying-in room, I suppose?" said Mr Bumble, not quite following the stranger's excited description.

"Yes," said the stranger. "A boy was born there."

"A many boys," observed Mr Bumble, shaking his head, despondingly.

"A murrain on the young devils!" cried the stranger; "I speak of one; a meek-looking, pale-faced boy, who was apprenticed down here, to a coffin-maker – I wish he had made his coffin, and screwed his body in it – and who afterwards ran away to London, as it was supposed."

"Why, you mean Oliver! Young Twist!" said Mr Bumble; "I remember him, of course. There wasn't a obstinater young rascal—"

"It's not of him I want to hear; I've heard enough of him," said the stranger, stopping Mr Bumble in the outset of a tirade on the subject of poor Oliver's vices. "It's of a woman; the hag that nursed his mother. Where is she?"

"Where is she?" said Mr Bumble, whom the gin-and-water had rendered facetious. "It would be hard to tell. There's no midwifery there, whichever place she's gone to; so I suppose she's out of employment, anyway."

"What do you mean?" demanded the stranger, sternly.

"That she died last winter," rejoined Mr Bumble.

The man looked fixedly at him when he had given this information, and although he did not withdraw his eyes for some time afterwards, his gaze gradually became vacant and abstracted, and he seemed lost in thought. For some time, he appeared doubtful whether he ought to be relieved or disappointed by the intelligence; but at length he breathed more freely; and withdrawing his eyes, observed that it was no great matter. With that he rose, as if to depart.

But Mr Bumble was cunning enough; and he at once saw that an opportunity was opened, for the lucrative disposal of some secret in the possession of his better half. He well remembered the night of old Sally's death, which the occurrences of that day had given him good reason to recollect, as the occasion on which he had proposed to Mrs Corney; and although that lady had never confided to him the disclosure of which she had been the solitary witness, he had heard enough to know that it related to something that had occurred in the old woman's attendance, as workhouse nurse, upon the young mother of Oliver Twist. Hastily calling this circumstance to mind, he informed the stranger, with an air of mystery, that one woman had been closeted with the old harridan shortly before she died; and that she could, as he had reason to believe, throw some light on the subject of his inquiry.

"How can I find her?" said the stranger, thrown off his guard; and plainly showing that all his fears (whatever they were) were aroused afresh by the intelligence.

"Only through me," rejoined Mr Bumble.

"When?" cried the stranger, hastily.

"Tomorrow," rejoined Bumble.

"At nine in the evening," said the stranger, producing a scrap of paper, and writing down upon it, an obscure address by the water-side. Shortly remarking that their roads were different, he departed, without more

ceremony than an emphatic repetition of the hour of appointment for the following night.

On glancing at the address, the parochial functionary observed that it contained no name. The stranger had not gone far, so he made after him to ask it.

"What do you want?" cried the man, turning quickly round, as Bumble touched him on the arm. "Following me!"

"Only to ask a question," said the other, pointing to the scrap of paper. "What name am I to ask for?"

"Monks!" rejoined the man; and strode hastily away.

CHAPTER 29

CONTAINING AN ACCOUNT OF WHAT PASSED BETWEEN MR AND MRS BUMBLE, AND MR MONKS, AT THEIR NOCTURNAL INTERVIEW

It was a dull, close, overcast summer evening. The clouds, which had been threatening all day, spread out in a dense and sluggish mass of vapour, already yielded large drops of rain, and seemed to presage a violent thunderstorm, when Mr and Mrs Bumble, turning out of the main street of the town, directed their course towards a scattered little colony of ruinous houses, distant from it some mile and a half, or thereabouts, and erected on a low unwholesome swamp, bordering upon the river.

In the heart of this cluster of huts; and skirting the river, which its upper stories overhung; stood a large building, formerly used as a manufactory of some kind.

It was before this ruinous building that the worthy couple paused, as the first peal of distant thunder reverberated in the air, and the rain commenced pouring violently down.

"The place should be somewhere here," said Bumble, consulting a scrap of paper he held in his hand.

"Halloa there!" cried a voice from above.

Following the sound, Mr Bumble raised his head and descried a man looking out of a door, breast-high, on the second story.

"Stand still, a minute," cried the voice; "I'll be with you directly." With which the head disappeared, and the door closed.

"Is that the man?" asked Mr Bumble's good lady.

Mr Bumble nodded in the affirmative.

"Then, mind what I told you," said the matron: "and be careful to say as little as you can, or you'll betray us at once."

Mr Bumble, who had eyed the building with very rueful looks, was apparently about to express some doubts relative to the advisability of proceeding any further with the enterprise just then, when he was prevented by the appearance of Monks: who opened a small door, near

which they stood, and beckoned them inwards.

"Come in!" he cried impatiently, stamping his foot upon the ground. "Don't keep me here!"

The woman, who had hesitated at first, walked boldly in, without any other invitation. Mr Bumble, who was ashamed or afraid to lag behind, followed: obviously very ill at ease and with scarcely any of that remarkable dignity which was usually his chief characteristic.

"What the devil made you stand lingering there, in the wet?" said Monks, turning round, and addressing Bumble, after he had bolted the door behind them.

"We – we were only cooling ourselves," stammered Bumble, looking apprehensively about him.

"Cooling yourselves!" retorted Monks. "Not all the rain that ever fell, or ever will fall, will put as much of hell's fire out, as a man can carry about with him. You won't cool yourself so easily; don't think it!"

With this agreeable speech, Monks turned short upon the matron, and bent his gaze upon her, till even she, who was not easily cowed, was fain to withdraw her eyes, and turn them towards the ground.

"This is the woman, is it?" demanded Monks.

"Hem! That is the woman," replied Mr Bumble, mindful of his wife's caution.

"You think women never can keep secrets, I suppose?" said the matron, interposing, and returning, as she spoke, the searching look of Monks.

"I know they will always keep *one* till it's found out," said Monks.

"And what may that be?" asked the matron.

"The loss of their own good name," replied Monks. "So, by the same rule, if a woman's a party to a secret that might hang or transport her, I'm not afraid of her telling it to anybody; not I! Do you understand, mistress?"

"No," rejoined the matron, slightly colouring as she spoke.

"Of course you don't!" said Monks. "How should you?"

Bestowing something halfway between a smile and a frown upon his two companions, and again beckoning them to follow him, the man hastened across the apartment, which was of considerable extent, but low in the roof. He was preparing to ascend a steep staircase, or rather ladder, leading to another floor of warehouses above: when a bright flash of lightning streamed down the aperture, and a peal of thunder followed, which shook the crazy building to its centre.

"Hear it!" he cried, shrinking back. "Hear it! Rolling and crashing on as if it echoed through a thousand caverns where the devils were hiding from it. I hate the sound!"

He remained silent for a few moments; and then, removing his hands suddenly from his face, showed, to the unspeakable discomposure of Mr Bumble, that it was much distorted, and discoloured.

"These fits come over me now and then," said Monks, observing his alarm; "and thunder sometimes brings them on. Don't mind me now; it's all over for this once."

Thus speaking, he led the way up the ladder; and hastily closing the window-shutters of the room into which it led, lowered a lantern which hung at the end of a rope and pulley passed through one of the heavy beams in the ceiling: and which cast a dim light upon an old table and three chairs that were placed beneath it.

"Now," said Monks, when they had all three seated themselves, "the sooner we come to our business, the better for all. The woman knows what it is, does she?"

The question was addressed to Bumble; but his wife anticipated the reply, by intimating that she was perfectly acquainted with it.

"He is right in saying that you were with this hag the night she died; and that she told you something—"

"About the mother of the boy you named," replied the matron, interrupting him. "Yes."

"The first question is, of what nature was her communication?" said Monks.

"That's the second," observed the woman with much deliberation. "The first is, what may the communication be worth?"

"Who the devil can tell that, without knowing of what kind it is?" asked Monks.

"Nobody better than you, I am persuaded," answered Mrs Bumble: who did not want for spirit, as her yoke-fellow could abundantly testify.

"Humph!" said Monks significantly, and with a look of eager inquiry; "there may be money's worth to get, eh?"

"Perhaps there may," was the composed reply.

"Something that was taken from her," said Monks. "Something that she wore. Something that—"

"You had better bid," interrupted Mrs Bumble. "I have heard enough, already, to assure me that you are the man I ought to talk to."

Mr Bumble, who had not yet been admitted by his better half into any greater share of the secret than he had originally possessed, listened to this dialogue with outstretched neck and distended eyes: which he directed towards his wife and Monks by turns, in undisguised astonishment; increased, if possible, when the latter sternly demanded what sum was required for the disclosure.

"What's it worth to you?" asked the woman, as collectedly as before.

"It may be nothing; it may be twenty pounds," replied Monks. "Speak out, and let me know which."

"Add five pounds to the sum you have named; give me five-and-twenty pounds in gold," said the woman; "and I'll tell you all I know. Not before."

"Five-and-twenty pounds!" exclaimed Monks, drawing back.

"I spoke as plainly as I could," replied Mrs Bumble. "It's not a large sum, either."

"Not a large sum for a paltry secret, that may be nothing when it's told!" cried Monks impatiently; "and which has been lying dead for twelve years past or more!"

"Such matters keep well, and, like good wine, often double their value in course of time," answered the matron, still preserving the resolute indifference she had assumed. "As to lying dead, there are those who will lie dead for twelve thousand years to come, or twelve million, for anything you or I know, who will tell strange tales at last!"

"What if I pay it for nothing?" asked Monks, hesitating.

"You can easily take it away again," replied the matron. "I am but a woman; alone here; and unprotected."

"Not alone, my dear, nor unprotected neither," submitted Mr Bumble, in a voice tremulous with fear: "*I* am here, my dear."

"You are a fool," said Mrs Bumble, in reply; "and had better hold your tongue."

"He had better have cut it out, before he came, if he can't speak in a lower tone," said Monks, grimly. "So! He's your husband, eh?"

"He my husband!" tittered the matron, parrying the question.

"I thought as much, when you came in," rejoined Monks, marking the angry glance which the lady darted at her spouse as she spoke. "So much the better; I have less hesitation in dealing with two people, when I find that there's only one will between them. I'm in earnest. See here!"

He thrust his hand into a side-pocket; and producing a canvas bag, told out twenty-five sovereigns on the table, and pushed them over to the woman.

"Now," he said, "gather them up; and when this cursed peal of thunder, which I feel is coming up to break over the house-top, is gone, let's hear your story."

The thunder having subsided, Monks bent forward to listen to what the woman should say.

"When this woman, that we called old Sally, died," the matron began, "she and I were alone."

"Was there no one by?" asked Monks, in the same hollow whisper; "no sick wretch or idiot in some other bed? No one who could hear, and might, by possibility, understand?"

"Not a soul," replied the woman; "we were alone. *I* stood alone beside the body when death came over it."

"Good," said Monks, regarding her attentively. "Go on."

"She spoke of a young creature," resumed the matron, "who had brought a child into the world some years before; not merely in the same room, but in the same bed, in which she then lay dying."

"Ay?" said Monks, with quivering lip, and glancing over his shoulder. "Blood! How things come about!"

"The child was the one you named to him last night," said the matron, nodding carelessly towards her husband; "the mother this nurse had robbed."

"In life?" asked Monks.

"In death," replied the woman, with something like a shudder. "She stole from the corpse, when it had hardly turned to one, that which the dead mother had prayed her, with her last breath, to keep for the infant's sake."

"She sold it?" cried Monks, with desperate eagerness; "did she sell it? Where? When? To whom? How long before?"

"As she told me, with great difficulty, that she had done this," said the matron, "she fell back and died."

"Without saying more?" cried Monks, in a voice which, from its very suppression, seemed only the more furious. "It's a lie! I'll not be played with. She said more. I'll tear the life out of you both, but I'll know what it was."

"She didn't utter another word," said the woman, to all appearance unmoved (as Mr Bumble was very far from being) by the strange man's violence; "but she clutched my gown, violently, with one hand, which was partly closed; and when I saw that she was dead, and so removed the hand by force, I found it clasped a scrap of dirty paper."

"Which contained—" interposed Monks, stretching forward.

"Nothing," replied the woman; "it was a pawnbroker's duplicate."

"For what?" demanded Monks.

"In good time I'll tell you," said the woman. "I judge that she had kept the trinket, for some time, in the hope of turning it to better account; and then had pawned it; and had saved or scraped together money to pay the pawnbroker's interest year by year, and prevent its running out; so that if anything came of it, it could still be redeemed. Nothing had come of it; and, as I tell you, she died with the scrap of paper, all worn and tattered, in her hand. The time was out in two days; I thought something might one day come of it too; and so redeemed the pledge."

"Where is it now?" asked Monks quickly.

"*There*," replied the woman. And, as if glad to be relieved of it, she hastily threw down upon the table a small kid bag scarcely large enough for a French watch, which Monks pouncing upon, tore open with trembling hands. It contained a little gold locket: in which were two locks of hair, and a plain gold wedding ring.

"It has the word 'Agnes' engraved on the inside," said the woman. "There is a blank left for the surname; and then follows the date; which is within a year before the child was born. I found out that."

"And this is all?" said Monks, after a close and eager scrutiny of the contents of the little packet.

"All," replied the woman.

Mr Bumble drew a long breath, as if he were glad to find that the story was over, and no mention made of taking the five-and-twenty pounds back again; and now he took courage to wipe off the perspiration which had been trickling over his nose, unchecked, during the whole of the previous dialogue.

"I know nothing of the story, beyond what I can guess at," said his wife, addressing Monks after a short silence; "and I want to know nothing; for it's safer not. But I may ask you two questions, may I?"

"You may ask," said Monks, with some show of surprise; "but whether I answer or not is another question."

" – Which makes three," observed Mr Bumble, essaying a stroke of facetiousness.

"Is that what you expected to get from me?" demanded the matron.

"It is," replied Monks. "The other question?"

"What do you propose to do with it? Can it be used against me?"

"Never," rejoined Monks; "nor against me either. See here! But don't move a step forward, or your life is not worth a bulrush."

With these words, he suddenly wheeled the table aside, and pulling an iron ring in the boarding, threw back a large trap-door, which opened close at Mr Bumble's feet, and caused that gentleman to retire several paces backward, with great precipitation.

"Look down," said Monks, lowering the lantern into the gulf. "Don't fear me. I could have let you down, quietly enough, when you were seated over it, if that had been my game."

Thus encouraged, the matron drew near to the brink; and even Mr Bumble himself, impelled by curiousity, ventured to do the same. The turbid water, swollen by the heavy rain, was rushing rapidly on below; and all other sounds were lost in the noise of its plashing and eddying against the green and slimy piles. There had once been a water-mill beneath; the tide, foaming and chafing round the few rotten stakes, and fragments of machinery that yet remained, seemed to dart onward, with a new impulse, when free from the obstacles which had unavailingly attempted to stem its headlong course.

"If you flung a man's body down there, where would it be tomorrow morning?" said Monks, swinging the lantern to and fro in the dark well.

"Twelve miles down the river, and cut to pieces besides," replied Bumble, recoiling at the thought.

Monks drew the little packet from his breast, where he had hurriedly thrust it; and tying it to a leaden weight, which had formed a part of some pulley, and was lying on the floor, dropped it into the stream. It fell straight, and true as a die; clove the water with a scarcely audible splash; and was gone.

The three looking into each other's faces, seemed to breathe more freely.

"There!" said Monks, closing the trapdoor, which fell heavily back into its former position. "If the sea ever gives up its dead, as books say it will, it will keep its gold and silver to itself, and that trash among it. We have nothing more to say, and may break up our pleasant party."

"By all means," observed Mr Bumble, with great alacrity.

"You'll keep a quiet tongue in your head, will you?" said Monks, with a threatening look. "I am not afraid of your wife."

"You may depend upon me, young man," answered Mr Bumble, bowing himself gradually towards the ladder, with excessive politeness. "On everybody's account, young man; on my own, you know, Mr Monks."

"I am glad, for your sake, to hear it," remarked Monks. "Light your lantern! And get away from here as fast as you can."

CHAPTER 30

INTRODUCES SOME RESPECTABLE CHARACTERS WITH WHOM THE READER IS ALREADY ACQUAINTED

On the evening following that upon which the three worthies mentioned in the last chapter, disposed of their little matter of business as therein narrated, Mr William Sikes, awakened from a nap, drowsily growled forth an inquiry of what time of night it was. Illness had not improved Mr Sikes's temper; for, as the girl raised him up and led him to a chair, he muttered various curses on her awkwardness, and struck her.

"Whining, are you?" said Sikes. "Come! Don't stand snivelling there. If you can't do anything better than that, cut off altogether. D'ye hear me?"

"I hear you," replied the girl, turning her face aside, and forcing a laugh. "What fancy have you got in your head now?"

"Oh! you've thought better of it, have you?" growled Sikes, marking the tear which trembled in her eye. "All the better for you, you have."

"Why, you don't mean to say, you'd be hard upon me tonight, Bill," said the girl, laying her hand upon his shoulder.

"No!" cried Mr Sikes. "Why not?"

"Such a number of nights," said the girl, with a touch of woman's tenderness, which communicated something like sweetness of tone, even to her voice: "such a number of nights as I've been patient with you, nursing and caring for you, as if you had been a child: and this the first that I've seen you like yourself; you wouldn't have served me as you did just now, if you'd thought of that, would you? Come, come; say you wouldn't."

"Well, then," rejoined Mr Sikes, "I wouldn't. Why, damme, now, the girl's whining again!"

"It's nothing," said the girl, throwing herself into a chair. "Don't you seem to mind me. It'll soon be over."

"Now," said the robber, "come and sit aside of me, and put on your own face; or I'll alter it so, that you won't know it again when you *do* want it."

The girl obeyed. Sikes, locking her hand in his, fell back upon the pillow: turning his eyes upon her face. They closed; opened again; closed once more; again opened. He shifted his position restlessly; and, after dozing again, and again, for two or three minutes, and as often springing up with a look of terror, and gazing vacantly about him, was suddenly stricken, as it were, while in the very attitude of rising, into a deep and heavy sleep. The grasp of his hand relaxed; the upraised arm fell languidly by his side; and he lay like one in a profound trance.

"The laudanum has taken effect at last," murmured the girl, as she rose from the bedside. "I may be too late, even now."

She hastily dressed herself in her bonnet and shawl; looking fearfully round, from time to time, as if, despite the sleeping draught, she expected every moment to feel the pressure of Sikes's heavy hand upon her shoulder; then, stooping softly over the bed, she kissed the robber's lips; and then opening and closing the room-door with noiseless touch, hurried from the house.

A watchman was crying half-past nine, down a dark passage through which she had to pass, in gaining the main thoroughfare.

"Has it long gone the half-hour?" asked the girl.

"It'll strike the hour in another quarter," said the man: raising his lantern to her face.

"And I cannot get there in less than an hour or more," muttered Nancy: brushing swiftly past him, and gliding rapidly down the street.

Many of the shops were already closing in the back lanes and avenues through which she tracked her way, in making from Spitalfields towards the West End of London. The clock struck ten, increasing her impatience. She tore along the narrow pavement: elbowing the passengers from side to side; and darting almost under the horses' heads, crossed crowded streets, where clusters of persons were eagerly watching their opportunity to do the like.

"The woman is mad!" said the people, turning to look after her as she rushed away.

When she reached the more wealthy quarter of the town, the streets were comparatively deserted; and here her headlong progress excited a still greater curiosity in the stragglers whom she hurried past. Some quickened their pace behind, as though to see whither she was hastening at such an unusual rate; and a few made head upon her, and looked back, surprised at her undiminished speed; but they fell off one by one; and when she neared her place of destination, she was alone.

It was a family hotel in a quiet but handsome street near Hyde Park. As the brilliant light of the lamp which burnt before its door, guided her to the spot, the clock struck eleven. She had loitered for a few paces as though irresolute, and making up her mind to advance; but the sound determined her, and she stepped into the hall. The porter's seat was vacant. She looked round with an air of incertitude, and advanced towards the stairs.

"Now, young woman!" said a smartly-dressed female, looking out from a door behind her, "who do you want here?"

"A lady who is stopping in this house," answered the girl.

"A lady!" was the reply, accompanied with a scornful look. "What lady?"

"Miss Maylie," said Nancy.

The young woman, who had by this time noted her appearance, replied only by a look of virtuous disdain; and summoned a man to answer her. To him, Nancy repeated her request.

"What name am I to say?" asked the waiter.

"It's of no use saying any," replied Nancy.

"Nor business?" said the man.

"No, nor that neither," rejoined the girl. "I must see the lady."

"Come!" said the man, pushing her towards the door. "None of this. Take yourself off."

"I shall be carried out, if I go!" said the girl violently; "and I can make that a job that two of you won't like to do. Isn't there anybody here," she said, looking round, "that will see a simple message carried for a poor wretch like me?"

This appeal produced an effect on a good-tempered-faced man-cook, who with some of the other servants was looking on, and who stepped forward to interfere.

"Take it up for her, Joe; can't you?" said this person.

"What's the good?" replied the man. "You don't suppose the young lady will see such as her; do you?"

This allusion to Nancy's doubtful character, raised a vast quantity of chaste wrath in the bosoms of four housemaids, who remarked, with great fervour, that the creature was a disgrace to her sex; and strongly advocated her being thrown, ruthlessly, into the kennel.

"Do what you like with me," said the girl, turning to the men again; "but do what I ask you first, and I ask you to give this message for God Almighty's sake."

The soft-hearted cook added his intercession, and the result was that the man who had first appeared undertook its delivery.

"What's it to be?" said the man, with one foot on the stairs.

"That a young woman earnestly asks to speak to Miss Maylie alone," said Nancy; "and that if the lady will only hear the first word she has to say, she will know whether to hear her business, or to have her turned out of doors as an impostor."

"I say," said the man, "you're coming it strong!"

"You give the message," said the girl firmly: "and let me hear the answer."

The man ran upstairs. Nancy remained, pale and almost breathless, listening with quivering lip to the very audible expressions of scorn, of which the chaste housemaids were very prolific; and of which they became still more so, when the man returned, and said the young woman was to walk upstairs.

"It's no good being proper in this world," said the first housemaid.

"Brass can do better than the gold what has stood the fire," said the second.

The third contented herself with wondering "what ladies was made of"; and the fourth took the first in a quartette of "Shameful!" with which the Dianas concluded.

Regardless of all this: for she had weightier matters at heart: Nancy followed the man, with trembling limbs, to a small antechamber, lighted by a lamp from the ceiling. Here he left her, and retired.

CHAPTER 31

A STRANGE INTERVIEW, WHICH IS A SEQUEL TO THE LAST CHAPTER

Nancy raised her eyes sufficiently to observe that the figure which presented itself was that of a slight and beautiful girl; then, bending them on the ground, she tossed her head with affected carelessness as she said:

"It's a hard matter to get to see you, lady. If I had taken offence, and gone away, as many would have done, you'd have been sorry for it one day, and not without reason either."

"I am very sorry if any one has behaved harshly to you," replied Rose. "Do not think of that. Tell me why you wished to see me. I am the person you inquired for."

The kind tone of this answer, the sweet voice, the gentle manner, the absence of any accent of haughtiness or displeasure, took the girl completely by surprise, and she burst into tears.

"Oh, lady, lady!" she said, clasping her hands passionately before her face, "if there was more like you, there would be fewer like me – there would – there would!"

"Sit down," said Rose, earnestly. "If you are in poverty or affliction I shall be truly glad to relieve you if I can – I shall indeed. Sit down."

"Let me stand, lady," said the girl, still weeping, "and do not speak to me so kindly till you know me better. It is growing late. Is – is – that door shut?"

"Yes," said Rose, recoiling a few steps, as if to be nearer assistance in case she should require it. "Why?"

"Because," said the girl, "I am about to put my life, and the lives of others in your hands. I am the girl that dragged little Oliver back to old Fagin's, on the night he went out from the house in Pentonville."

"You!" said Rose Maylie.

"I, lady!" replied the girl. "I am the infamous creature you have heard of, that lives among the thieves, and that never from the first moment I can recollect my eyes and senses opening on London streets have known any better life, or kinder words than they have given me, so help me God! Do not mind shrinking openly from me, lady. I am younger than you would think, to look at me, but I am well used to it. The poorest women fall back, as I make my way along the crowded pavement."

"What dreadful things are these!" said Rose, involuntarily falling from her strange companion.

"Thank Heaven upon your knees, dear lady," cried the girl, "that you had friends to care for and keep you in your childhood, and that you were never in the midst of cold and hunger, and riot and drunkenness, and – and – something worse than all – as I have been from my cradle. I may use the word, for the alley and the gutter were mine, as they will be my deathbed."

"I pity you!" said Rose, in a broken voice. "It wrings my heart to hear you!"

"Heaven bless you for your goodness!" rejoined the girl. "If you knew what I am sometimes, you would pity me, indeed. But I have stolen away from those who would surely murder me, if they knew I had been here, to tell you what I have overheard. Do you know a man named Monks?"

"No," said Rose.

"He knows you," replied the girl; "and knew you were here, for it was by hearing him tell the place that I found you out."

"I never heard the name," said Rose.

"Then he goes by some other amongst us," rejoined the girl, "which I more than thought before. Some time ago, and soon after Oliver was put into your house on the night of the robbery, I – suspecting this man – listened to a conversation held between him and Fagin in the dark. I found out, from what I heard, that Monks – the man I asked you about, you know—"

"Yes," said Rose, "I understand."

"—That Monks," pursued the girl, "had seen him accidentally with two of our boys on the day we first lost him, and had known him directly to be the same child that he was watching for, though I couldn't make out why. A bargain was struck with Fagin, that if Oliver was got back he should have a certain sum; and he was to have more for making him a thief, which this Monks wanted for some purpose of his own."

"For what purpose?" asked Rose.

"He caught sight of my shadow on the wall as I listened, in the hope of finding out," said the girl; "and there are not many people besides me that could have got out of their way in time to escape discovery. But I did; and I saw him no more till last night."

"And what occurred then?"

"I'll tell you, lady. Last night he came again. Again they went upstairs, and I, wrapping myself up so that my shadow would not betray me, again listened at the door. The first words I heard Monks say were these:

'So the only proofs of the boy's identity lie at the bottom of the river, and the old hag that received them from the mother is rotting in her coffin.' They laughed, and talked of his success in doing this; and Monks, talking on about the boy and getting very wild, said that though he had got the young devil's money safely now, he'd rather have had it the other way; for, what a game it would have been to have brought down the boast of the father's will, by driving him through every jail in town, and then hauling him up for some capital felony which Fagin could easily manage, after having made a good profit of him besides."

"What is all this!" said Rose.

"The truth, lady, though it comes from my lips," replied the girl. "Then, he said, with oaths common enough to my ears, but strange to yours, that if he could gratify his hatred by taking the boy's life without bringing his own neck in danger, he would; but, as he couldn't, he'd be upon the watch to meet him at every turn in life; and if he took advantage of his birth and history, he might harm him yet. 'In short, Fagin,' he says, 'scoundrel as you are, you never laid such snares as I'll contrive for my young brother, Oliver.'"

"His brother!" exclaimed Rose.

"Those were his words," said Nancy, glancing uneasily round, as she had scarcely ceased to do, since she began to speak, for a vision of Sikes haunted her perpetually. "And more. When he spoke of you and the other lady, and said it seemed contrived by Heaven, or the devil, against him, that Oliver should come into your hands, he laughed, and said there was some comfort in that too, for how many thousands and hundreds of thousands of pounds would you not give, if you had them, to know who your two-legged spaniel was."

"You do not mean," said Rose, turning very pale, "to tell me that this was said in earnest?"

"He spoke in hard and angry earnest, if a man ever did," replied the girl, shaking her head. "He is an earnest man when his hatred is up. I know many who do worse things; but I'd rather listen to them all a dozen times, than to that Monks once. It is growing late, and I have to reach home without suspicion of having been on such an errand as this. I must get back quickly."

"But what can I do?" said Rose. "To what use can I turn this communication without you? Back! Why do you wish to return to companions you paint in such terrible colours? If you repeat this information to a gentleman whom I can summon in an instant from the next room, you can be consigned to some place of safety without half an hour's delay."

"I wish to go back," said the girl. "I must go back, because – how can I tell such things to an innocent lady like you? – because among the men I have told you of, there is one: the most desperate among them all: that I can't leave; no, not even to be saved from the life I am leading now."

"Your having interfered in this dear boy's behalf before," said Rose; "your coming here, at so great a risk, to tell me what you have heard; your manner, which convinces me of the truth of what you say; your evident contrition, and sense of shame; all lead me to believe that you might be yet reclaimed. Oh!" said the earnest girl, folding her hands as the tears coursed down her face, "do not turn a deaf ear to the entreaties of one of your own sex; the first – the first, I do believe, who ever appealed to you in the voice of pity and compassion. Do hear my words, and let me save you yet, for better things."

"Lady," cried the girl, sinking on her knees, "dear, sweet, angel lady, you *are* the first that ever blessed me with such words as these, and if I had heard them years ago, they might have turned me from

a life of sin and sorrow; but it is too late, it is too late!"

"It is never too late," said Rose, "for penitence and atonement."

"It is," cried the girl, writhing in the agony of her mind; "I cannot leave him now! I could not be his death."

"Why should you be?" asked Rose.

"Nothing could save him," cried the girl. "If I told others what I have told you, and led to their being taken, he would be sure to die. He is the boldest, and has been so cruel!"

"Is it possible," cried Rose, "that for such a man as this, you can resign every future hope, and the certainty of immediate rescue? It is madness."

"I don't know what it is," answered the girl; "I only know that it is so, and not with me alone, but with hundreds of others as bad and wretched as myself. I must go back. Whether it is God's wrath for the wrong I have done, I do not know; but I am drawn back to him through every suffering and ill usage; and I should be, I believe, if I knew that I was to die by his hand at last."

"What am I to do?" said Rose. "I should not let you depart from me thus."

"You should, lady, and I know you will," rejoined the girl, rising. "You will not stop my going because I have trusted in your goodness, and forced no promise from you, as I might have done."

"Of what use, then, is the communication you have made?" said Rose. "This mystery must be investigated, or how will its disclosure to me, benefit Oliver, whom you are anxious to serve?"

"You must have some kind gentleman about you that will hear it as a secret, and advise you what to do," rejoined the girl.

"But where can I find you again when it is necessary?" asked Rose. "I do not seek to know where these dreadful people live, but where will you be walking or passing at any settled period from this time?"

"Will you promise me that you will have my secret strictly kept, and come alone, or with the only other person that knows it; and that I shall not be watched or followed?" asked the girl.

"I promise you solemnly," answered Rose.

"Every Sunday night, from eleven until the clock strikes twelve," said the girl without hesitation, "I will walk on London Bridge if I am alive."

"Stay another moment," interposed Rose, as the girl moved hurriedly towards the door. "Think once again on your own condition, and the opportunity you have of escaping from it. You have a claim on me: not only as the voluntary bearer of this intelligence, but as a woman lost almost beyond redemption. Will you return to this gang of robbers, and to this man, when a word can save you? What fascination is it that can take you back, and make you cling to wickedness and misery? Oh! is there no chord in your heart that I can touch! Is there nothing left, to which I can appeal against this terrible infatuation!"

"When ladies as young, and good, and beautiful as you are," replied the girl steadily, "give away your hearts, love will carry you all lengths – even such as you, who have home, friends, other admirers, everything, to fill them. When such as I, who have no certain roof but the coffin-lid, and no friend in sickness or death but the hospital nurse, set our rotten hearts on any man, and let him fill the place that has been a blank through all our wretched lives, who can hope to cure us? Pity us, lady – pity us for having only one feeling of the woman left, and for having that turned, by a heavy judgment, from a comfort and a pride, into a new means of violence and suffering."

"You will," said Rose, after a pause, "take some money from me, which may enable you to live without dishonesty – at all events until we meet again?"

"Not a penny," replied the girl, waving her hand.

"Do not close your heart against all my efforts to help you," said Rose, stepping gently forward. "I wish to serve you indeed."

"You would serve me best, lady," replied the girl, wringing her hands, "if you could take my life at once; for I have felt more grief to think of what I am, tonight, than I ever did before, and it would be something not to die in the hell in which I have lived. God bless you, sweet lady, and send as much happiness on your head as I have brought shame on mine!"

Thus speaking, and sobbing aloud, the unhappy creature turned away; while Rose Maylie, overpowered by this extraordinary interview, which had more the semblance of a rapid dream than an actual occurrence, sank into a chair, and endeavoured to collect her wandering thoughts.

CHAPTER 32

CONTAINING FRESH DISCOVERIES, AND SHOWING THAT SURPRISES, LIKE MISFORTUNES, SELDOM COME ALONE

They purposed remaining in London only three days, prior to departing for some weeks to a distant part of the coast. It was now midnight of the first day. What course of action could she determine upon, which could be adopted in eight-and-forty hours? Or how could she postpone the journey without exciting suspicion?

Mr Losberne was with them, and would be for the next two days; but Rose was too well acquainted with the excellent gentleman's impetuosity, and foresaw too clearly the wrath with which, in the first explosion of his indignation, he would regard the instrument of Oliver's recapture, to trust him with the secret, when her representations in the girl's behalf could be seconded by no experienced person.

Disturbed by these different reflections; inclining now to one course and then to another, and again recoiling from all, as each successive consideration presented itself to her mind; Rose passed a sleepless and anxious night.

The next day, Oliver, who had been walking in the streets, with Mr Giles for a bodyguard, entered her room in such breathless haste and violent agitation, as seemed to betoken some new cause of alarm.

"What makes you look so flurried?" asked Rose, advancing to meet him.

"I hardly know how; I feel as if I should be choked," replied the boy. "Oh dear! To think that I should see him at last, and you should be able to know that I have told you all the truth!"

"I never thought you had told us anything but the truth," said Rose, soothing him. "But what is this? – of whom do you speak?"

"I have seen the gentleman," replied Oliver, scarcely able to articulate, "the gentleman who was so good to me – Mr Brownlow, that we have so often talked about."

"Where?" asked Rose.

"Getting out of a coach," replied Oliver, shedding tears of delight, "and going into a house. I didn't speak to him – I couldn't speak to him, for he didn't see me, and I trembled so, that I was not able to go up to him. But Giles asked, for me, whether he lived there, and they said he did. Look here," said Oliver, opening a scrap of paper, "here it is; here's where he lives – I'm going there directly! Oh, dear me, dear me! What shall I do when I come to see him and hear him speak again!"

With her attention not a little distracted by these and a great many other incoherent exclamations of joy, Rose read the address, which was Craven Street, in the Strand. She very soon determined upon turning the discovery to account.

"Quick!" she said. "Tell them to fetch a hackney-coach, and be ready to go with me. I will take you there directly, without a minute's loss of time. I will only tell my aunt that we are going out for an hour, and be ready as soon as you are."

Oliver needed no prompting to dispatch, and in little more than five minutes they were on their way to Craven Street. When they arrived there, Rose left Oliver in the coach, under pretence of preparing the

old gentleman to receive him; and sending up her card by the servant, requested to see Mr Brownlow on very pressing business. The servant soon returned, to beg that she would walk upstairs; and following him into an upper room, Miss Maylie was presented to an elderly gentleman of benevolent appearance, in a bottle-green coat. At no great distance from whom, was seated another old gentleman, in nankeen breeches and gaiters; who did not look particularly benevolent, and who was sitting with his hands clasped on the top of a thick stick, and his chin propped thereupon.

"Dear me," said the gentleman, in the bottle-green coat, hastily rising with great politeness, "I beg your pardon, young lady – I imagined it was some importunate person who – I beg you will excuse me. Be seated, pray."

"Mr Brownlow, I believe, sir?" said Rose, glancing from the other gentleman to the one who had spoken.

"That is my name," said the old gentleman. "This is my friend, Mr Grimwig. Grimwig, will you leave us for a few minutes?"

"I believe," interposed Miss Maylie, "that at this period of our interview, I need not give that gentleman the trouble of going away. If I am correctly informed, he is cognizant of the business on which I wish to speak to you."

Mr Brownlow inclined his head. Mr Grimwig, who had made one very stiff bow, and risen from his chair, made another very stiff bow, and dropped into it again.

"I shall surprise you very much, I have no doubt," said Rose, naturally embarrassed; "but you once showed great benevolence and goodness to a very dear young friend of mine, and I am sure you will take an interest in hearing of him again."

"Indeed!" said Mr Brownlow.

"Oliver Twist you knew him as," replied Rose.

The words no sooner escaped her lips, than Mr Grimwig, who had been affecting to dip into a large book that lay on the table, upset it with a great crash, and falling back in his chair, discharged from his features every expression but one of unmitigated wonder, and indulged in a prolonged and vacant stare; then, as if ashamed of having betrayed so much emotion, he jerked himself, as it were, by a convulsion into his former attitude, and looking out straight before him emitted a long deep whistle, which seemed, at last, not to be discharged on empty air, but to die away in the innermost recesses of his stomach.

Mr Brownlow was no less surprised, although his astonishment was not expressed in the same eccentric manner. He drew his chair nearer to Miss Maylie's, and said,

"Do me the favour, my dear young lady, to leave entirely out of the question that goodness and benevolence of which you speak, and of which nobody else knows anything; and if you have it in your power to produce any evidence which will alter the unfavourable opinion I was once induced to entertain of that poor child, in Heaven's name put me in possession of it."

"A bad one! I'll eat my head if he is not a bad one," growled Mr Grimwig, speaking by some ventriloquial power, without moving a muscle of his face.

"He is a child of a noble nature and a warm heart," said Rose, colouring; "and that Power which has thought fit to try him beyond his years, has planted in his breast affections and feelings which would do honour to many who have numbered his days six times over."

"I'm only sixty-one," said Mr Grimwig, with the same rigid face. "And, as the devil's in it if this Oliver is not twelve years old at least, I don't see the application of that remark."

"Do not heed my friend, Miss Maylie," said Mr Brownlow; "he does not mean what he says."

"Yes, he does," growled Mr Grimwig.

"No, he does not," said Mr Brownlow, obviously rising in wrath as he spoke.

"He'll eat his head, if he doesn't," growled Mr Grimwig.

"He would deserve to have it knocked off, if he does," said Mr Brownlow.

"And he'd uncommonly like to see any man offer to do it," responded Mr Grimwig, knocking his stick upon the floor.

Having gone thus far, the two old gentlemen severally took snuff, and afterwards shook hands, according to their invariable custom.

"Now, Miss Maylie," said Mr Brownlow, "to return to the subject in which your humanity is so much interested. Will you let me know what intelligence you have of this poor child: allowing me to premise that I exhausted every means in my power of discovering him, and that since I have been absent from this country, my first impression that he had imposed upon me, and had been persuaded by his former associates to rob me, has been considerably shaken."

Rose, who had had time to collect her thoughts, at once related, in a few natural words, all that had befallen Oliver since he left Mr Brownlow's house; reserving Nancy's information for that gentleman's private ear, and concluding with the assurance that his only sorrow, for some months past, had been the not being able to meet with his former benefactor and friend.

"Thank God!" said the old gentleman. "This is great happiness to me, great happiness. But you have not told me where he is now, Miss Maylie. You must pardon my finding fault with you – but why not have brought him?"

"He is waiting in a coach at the door," replied Rose.

"At this door!" cried the old gentleman. With which he hurried out of the room, down the stairs, up the coachsteps, and into the coach, without another word.

When the room-door closed behind him, Mr Grimwig lifted up his head, and converting one of the hind legs of his chair into a pivot, described three distinct circles with the assistance of his stick and the table; sitting in it all the time. After performing this evolution, he rose and limped as fast as he could up and down the room at least a dozen times, and then stopping suddenly before Rose, kissed her without the slightest preface.

"Hush!" he said, as the young lady rose in some alarm at this unusual proceeding. "Don't be afraid. I'm old enough to be your grandfather. You're a sweet girl. I like you. Here they are!"

In fact, as he threw himself at one dexterous dive into his former seat, Mr Brownlow returned, accompanied by Oliver, whom Mr Grimwig received very graciously; and if the gratification of that moment had been the only reward for all her anxiety and care in Oliver's behalf, Rose Maylie would have been well repaid.

"There is somebody else who should not be forgotten, by the by," said Mr Brownlow, ringing the bell. "Send Mrs Bedwin here, if you please."

The old housekeeper answered the summons with all dispatch; and dropping a curtsey at the door, waited for orders.

"Why, you get blinder every day, Bedwin," said Mr Brownlow, rather testily.

"Well, that I do, sir," replied the old lady. "People's eyes, at my time of life, don't improve with age, sir."

"I could have told you that," rejoined Mr Brownlow; "but put on your glasses, and see if you can't find out what you were wanted for, will you?"

The old lady began to rummage in her pocket for her spectacles. But Oliver's patience was not proof against this new trial; and yielding to his first impulse, he sprang into her arms.

"God be good to me!" cried the old lady, embracing him; "it is my innocent boy!"

"My dear old nurse!" cried Oliver.

"He would come back – I knew he would," said the old lady, holding him in her arms. "How well he looks, and how like a gentleman's son he is dressed again! Where have you been, this long, long while? Ah! the same sweet face, but not so pale; the same soft eye, but not so sad. I have never forgotten them or his quiet smile, but have seen them every day, side by side with those of my own dear children, dead and gone since I was a lightsome young creature." Running on thus, and now holding Oliver from her to mark how he had grown, now clasping him to her and passing her fingers fondly through his hair, the good soul laughed and wept upon his neck by turns.

Leaving her and Oliver to compare notes at leisure, Mr Brownlow led the way into another room; and there, heard from Rose a full narration of her interview with Nancy, which occasioned him no little surprise and perplexity. Rose also explained her reasons for not confiding in her friend Mr Losberne in the first instance. The old gentleman considered that she had acted prudently, and readily undertook to hold solemn conference with the worthy doctor himself. To afford him an early opportunity for the execution of this design, it was arranged that he should call at the hotel at eight o'clock that evening, and that in the meantime Mrs Maylie should be cautiously informed of all that had occurred. These preliminaries adjusted, Rose and Oliver returned home.

Rose had by no means overrated the measure of the good doctor's wrath. Nancy's history was no sooner unfolded to him, than he poured forth a shower of mingled threats and execrations; threatened to make her the first victim of the combined ingenuity of Messrs Blathers and Duff; and actually put on his hat preparatory to sallying forth to obtain the assistance of those worthies. And, doubtless, he would, in this first outbreak, have carried the intention into effect without a moment's consideration of the consequences, if he had not been restrained, in part by corresponding violence on the side of Mr Brownlow, who was himself of an irascible temperament, and partly by such arguments and representations as seemed best calculated to dissuade him from his hotbrained purpose.

“Then what the devil is to be done?” said the impetuous doctor, when they had rejoined the two ladies. “Are we to pass a vote of thanks to all these vagabonds, male and female, and beg them to accept a hundred

pounds, or so, apiece, as a trifling mark of our esteem, and some slight acknowledgment of their kindness to Oliver?"

"Not exactly that," rejoined Mr Brownlow, laughing; "but we must proceed gently and with great care."

"Gentleness and care," exclaimed the doctor. "I'd send them one and all to—"

"Never mind where," interposed Mr Brownlow. "But reflect whether sending them anywhere is likely to attain the object we have in view."

"What object?" asked the doctor.

"Simply, the discovery of Oliver's parentage, and regaining for him the inheritance of which, if this story be true, he has been fraudulently deprived."

"Ah!" said Mr Losberne, cooling himself with his pocket-handkerchief; "I almost forgot that."

"You see," pursued Mr Brownlow; "placing this poor girl entirely out of the question, and supposing it were possible to bring these scoundrels to justice without compromising her safety, what good should we bring about?"

"Hanging a few of them at least, in all probability," suggested the doctor, "and transporting the rest."

"Very good," replied Mr Brownlow, smiling; "but no doubt they will bring that about for themselves in the fulness of time, and if we step in to forestall them, it seems to me that we shall be performing a very Quixotic act, in direct opposition to our own interest – or at least to Oliver's, which is the same thing."

"How?" inquired the doctor.

"Thus. It is quite clear that we shall have extreme difficulty in getting to the bottom of this mystery, unless we can bring this man, Monks, upon his knees. That can only be done by stratagem, and by catching him when he is not surrounded by these people. For, suppose he were apprehended, we have no proof against him. He is not even (so far as we know, or as the facts appear to us) concerned with the gang in any of their robberies. If he were not discharged, it is very unlikely that he could receive any further punishment than being committed to prison as a rogue and vagabond;

and of course ever afterwards his mouth would be so obstinately closed that he might as well, for our purposes, be deaf, dumb, blind, and an idiot."

"Then," said the doctor impetuously, "I put it to you again, whether you think it reasonable that this promise to the girl should be considered binding; a promise made with the best and kindest intentions, but really—"

"Do not discuss the point, my dear young lady, pray," said Mr Brownlow, interrupting Rose as she was about to speak. "The promise shall be kept. I don't think it will, in the slightest degree, interfere with our proceedings. But, before we can resolve upon any precise course of action, it will be necessary to see the girl; to ascertain from her whether she will point out this Monks, on the understanding that he is to be dealt with by us, and not by the law; or, if she will not, or cannot do that, to procure from her such an account of his haunts and description of his person, as will enable us to identify him. She cannot be seen until next Sunday night; this is Tuesday. I would suggest that in the meantime, we remain perfectly quiet, and keep these matters secret even from Oliver himself."

Although Mr Losberne received with many wry faces a proposal involving a delay of five whole days, he was fain to admit that no better course occurred to him just then; and as both Rose and Mrs Maylie sided very strongly with Mr Brownlow, that gentleman's proposition was carried unanimously.

CHAPTER 33

FATAL CONSEQUENCES

It was nearly two hours before day-break; that time which, in the autumn of the year, may be truly called the dead of night; when the streets are silent and deserted; when even sounds appear to slumber, and profligacy and riot have staggered home to dream; it was at this still and silent hour, that Fagin sat watching in his old lair, with face so distorted and pale, and eyes so red and bloodshot, that he looked less like a man, than like some hideous phantom, moist from the grave, and worried by an evil spirit.

He sat crouching over a cold hearth, wrapped in an old torn coverlet, with his face turned towards a wasting candle that stood upon a table by his side. His right hand was raised to his lips, and as, absorbed in thought, he bit his long black nails, he disclosed among his toothless gums a few such fangs as should have been a dog's or rat's.

He sat without changing his attitude in the least, or appearing to take the smallest heed of time, until his quick ear seemed to be attracted by a footstep in the street.

"At last," he muttered, wiping his dry and fevered mouth. "At last!"

The bell rang gently as he spoke. He crept upstairs to the door, and presently returned accompanied by a man muffled to the chin, who carried a bundle under one arm. Sitting down and throwing back his outer coat, the man displayed the burly frame of Sikes.

"There!" he said, laying the bundle on the table. "Take care of that, and do the most you can with it. It's been trouble enough to get; I thought I should have been here, three hours ago."

Fagin laid his hand upon the bundle, and locking it in the cupboard, sat down again without speaking. But he did not take his eyes off the robber, for an instant, during this action; and now that they sat over against each other, face to face, he looked fixedly at him, with his lips quivering so violently, and his face so altered by the emotions which had mastered him, that the housebreaker involuntarily drew back his chair, and surveyed him with a look of real affright.

"Wot now?" cried Sikes. "Wot do you look at a man so for?"

Fagin raised his right hand, and shook his trembling forefinger in the air; but his passion was so great, that the power of speech was for the moment gone.

"Damme!" said Sikes, feeling in his breast with a look of alarm. "He's gone mad. I must look to myself here."

"No, no," rejoined Fagin, finding his voice. "It's not – you're not the person, Bill. I've no – no fault to find with you."

"Oh, you haven't, haven't you?" said Sikes, looking sternly at him, and ostentatiously passing a pistol into a more convenient pocket. "That's lucky – for one of us. Which one that is, don't matter."

"I've got that to tell you, Bill," said Fagin, drawing his chair nearer, "will make you worse than me."

"Aye?" returned the robber with an incredulous air. "Tell away! Look sharp, or Nance will think I'm lost."

"Lost!" cried Fagin. "She has pretty well settled that, in her own mind, already."

Sikes looked with an aspect of great perplexity into the old man's face, and reading no satisfactory explanation of the riddle there, clenched his coat collar in his huge hand and shook him soundly.

"Speak, will you!" he said; "or if you don't, it shall be for want of breath. Open your mouth and say wot you've got to say in plain words. Out with it, you thundering old cur, out with it!"

"It's Nancy," said Fagin, clutching Sikes by the wrist, as if to prevent his leaving the house before he had heard enough. "I followed her to London Bridge, where she met two people. A gentleman and a lady that she had gone to of her own accord before, who asked her to give up all her pals, and Monks first, which she did – and to describe him, which she did – and to tell her what house it was that we meet at, and go to, which she did – and where it could be best watched from, which she did – and what

time the people went there, which she did. She did all this. She told it all every word without a threat, without a murmur – she did!" cried Fagin, half mad with fury.

"What did they say?"

"They asked her," said Fagin, who, as he grew more wakeful, seemed to have a dawning perception who Sikes was, "they asked her why she didn't come, last Sunday, as she promised. She said she couldn't."

"Why – why?"

"Because she was forcibly kept at home by Bill, the man she had told them of before."

"What more of him?" cried Sikes.

"Why, that she couldn't very easily get out of doors unless he knew where she was going to, so the first time she went to see the lady, she – ha! ha! ha! it made me laugh when she said it, that it did – she gave him a drink of laudanum."

"Hell's fire!" cried Sikes, breaking fiercely from Fagin. "Let me go!"

Flinging the old man from him, he rushed from the room, and darted, wildly and furiously, up the stairs.

"Bill, Bill!" cried Fagin, following him hastily. "A word. Only a word."

The word would not have been exchanged, but that the housebreaker was unable to open the door: on which he was expending fruitless oaths and violence, when the old man came panting up.

"Let me out," said Sikes. "Don't speak to me; it's not safe. Let me out, I say!"

"Hear me speak a word," rejoined Fagin, laying his hand upon the lock. "You won't be—"

"Well," replied the other.

"You won't be – too – violent, Bill?"

The day was breaking, and there was light enough for the men to see each other's faces. They exchanged one brief glance; there was a fire in the eyes of both, which could not be mistaken.

"I mean," said Fagin, showing that he felt all disguise was now useless, "not too violent for safety. Be crafty, Bill, and not too bold."

Sikes made no reply; but, pulling open the door, of which Fagin had turned the lock, dashed into the silent streets.

Without one pause, or moment's consideration; without once turning his head to the right or left, or raising his eyes to the sky, or lowering them to the ground, but looking straight before him with savage resolution: his teeth so tightly compressed that the strained jaw seemed starting through his skin; the robber held on his headlong course, nor muttered a word, nor relaxed a muscle, until he reached his own door. He opened it, softly, with a key; strode lightly up the stairs; and entering his own room, double-locked the door, and lifting a heavy table against it, drew back the curtain of the bed.

The girl was lying, half-dressed, upon it. He had roused her from her sleep, for she raised herself with a hurried and startled look.

"Get up!" said the man.

"It *is* you, Bill!" said the girl, with an expression of pleasure at his return.

"It is," was the reply. "Get up."

There was a candle burning, but the man hastily drew it from the candlestick, and hurled it under the grate. Seeing the faint light of early day without, the girl rose to undraw the curtain.

"Let it be," said Sikes, thrusting his hand before her. "There's enough light for wot I've got to do."

"Bill," said the girl, in the low voice of alarm, "why do you look like that at me!"

The robber sat regarding her, for a few seconds, with dilated nostrils and heaving breast; and then, grasping her by the head and throat, dragged her into the middle of the room, and looking once towards the door, placed his heavy hand upon her mouth.

"Bill, Bill!" gasped the girl, wrestling with the strength of mortal fear—"I— I won't scream or cry – not once – hear me – speak to me – tell me what I have done!"

"You know, you she devil!" returned the robber, suppressing his breath. "You were watched tonight; every word you said was heard."

"Then spare my life for the love of Heaven, as I spared yours," rejoined the girl, clinging to him. "Bill, dear Bill, you cannot have the heart to kill me. Oh! think of all I have given up, only this one night, for you. You *shall* have time to think, and save yourself this crime; I will not loose my hold, you cannot throw me off. Bill, Bill, for dear God's sake, for your own, for mine, stop before you spill my blood! I have been true to you, upon my guilty soul I have!"

The man struggled violently to release his arms; but those of the girl were clasped round his, and tear her as he would, he could not tear them away.

"Bill," cried the girl, striving to lay her head upon his breast, "the gentleman and that dear lady, told me tonight of a home in some foreign country where I could end my days in solitude and peace. Let me see them again, and beg them, on my knees, to show the same mercy and goodness to you; and let us both leave this dreadful place, and far apart lead better lives, and forget how we have lived, except in prayers, and never see each other more. It is never too late to repent. They told me so – I feel it now – but we must have time – a little, little time!"

The housebreaker freed one arm, and grasped his pistol. The certainty of immediate detection if he fired, flashed across his mind even in the midst of his fury; and he beat it twice with all the force he could summon, upon the upturned face that almost touched his own.

She staggered and fell: nearly blinded with the blood that rained down from a deep gash in her forehead.

It was a ghastly figure to look upon. The murderer staggering backward to the wall, and shutting out the sight with his hand, seized a heavy club and struck her down.

CHAPTER 34

MONKS AND MR BROWNLOW AT LENGTH MEET. THEIR CONVERSATION, AND THE INTELLIGENCE THAT INTERRUPTS IT

The twilight was beginning to close in, when Mr Brownlow alighted from a hackney-coach at his own door, and knocked softly. The door being opened, a sturdy man got out of the coach and stationed himself on one side of the steps, while another man, who had been seated on the box, dismounted too, and stood upon the other side. At a sign from Mr Brownlow, they helped out a third man, and taking him between them, hurried him into the house. This man was Monks.

They walked in the same manner up the stairs without speaking, and Mr Brownlow, preceding them, led the way into a back-room. At the door of this apartment, Monks, who had ascended with evident reluctance, stopped. The two men looked at the old gentleman as if for instructions.

"He knows the alternative," said Mr Brownlow. "If he hesitates or moves a finger but as you bid him, drag him into the street, call for the aid of the police, and impeach him as a felon in my name."

"How dare you say this of me?" asked Monks.

"How dare you urge me to it, young man?" replied Mr Brownlow, confronting him with a steady look. "Are you mad enough to leave this house? Unhand him. There, sir. You are free to go, and we to follow. But I warn you, by all I hold most solemn and most sacred, that the instant you set foot in the street, that instant will I have you apprehended on a charge of fraud and robbery. I am resolute and immoveable. If you are determined to be the same, your blood be upon your own head!"

"By what authority am I kidnapped in the street, and brought here by these dogs?" asked Monks, looking from one to the other of the men who stood beside him.

"By mine," replied Mr Brownlow. "Those persons are indemnified by me. If you complain of being deprived of your liberty – you had power and opportunity to retrieve it as you came along, but you deemed it advisable to remain quiet – I say again, throw yourself for protection on the law. I will appeal to the law too; but when you have gone too far to recede, do not sue to me for leniency, when the power will have passed into other hands; and do not say I plunged you down the gulf into which you rushed, yourself."

Monks was plainly disconcerted, and alarmed besides. He hesitated.

"You will decide quickly," said Mr Brownlow, with perfect firmness and composure. "If you wish me to prefer my charges publicly, and consign you to a punishment the extent of which, although I can, with a shudder, foresee, I cannot control, once more, I say, for you know the way. If not, and you appeal to my forbearance, and the mercy of those you have deeply injured, seat yourself, without a word, in that chair. It has waited for you two whole days."

Monks muttered some unintelligible words, but wavered still.

"You will be prompt," said Mr Brownlow. "A word from me, and the alternative has gone for ever."

Still the man hesitated.

"I have not the inclination to parley," said Mr Brownlow, "and, as I advocate the dearest interests of others, I have not the right."

"Is there—" demanded Monks with a faltering tongue— "is there— no middle course?"

"None."

Monks looked at the old gentleman, with an anxious eye; but, reading in his countenance nothing but severity and determination, walked into the room, and, shrugging his shoulders, sat down.

"Lock the door on the outside," said Mr Brownlow to the attendants, "and come when I ring."

The men obeyed, and the two were left alone together.

"This is pretty treatment, sir," said Monks, throwing down his hat and cloak, "from my father's oldest friend."

"It is because I was your father's oldest friend, young man," returned Mr Brownlow; "it is because the hopes and wishes of young and happy years were bound up with him, and that fair creature of his blood and kindred who rejoined her God in youth, and left me here a solitary, lonely man: it is because he knelt with me beside his only sister's death-bed when he was yet a boy, on the morning that would – but Heaven willed otherwise – have made her my young wife; it is because my seared heart clung to him, from that time forth, through all his trials and errors, till he died; it is because old recollections and associations filled my heart, and even the sight of you brings with it old thoughts of him; it is because of all these things that I am moved to treat you gently now – yes, Edward Leeford, even now – and blush for your unworthiness who bear the name."

"What has the name to do with it?" asked the other, after contemplating, half in silence, and half in dogged wonder, the agitation of his companion.

"What is the name to me?"

"Nothing," replied Mr Brownlow, "nothing to you. But it was *hers*, and even at this distance of time brings back to me, an old man, the glow and thrill which I once felt, only to hear it repeated by a stranger. I am very glad you have changed it – very – very."

"This is all mighty fine," said Monks (to retain his assumed designation) after a long silence, during which he had jerked himself in sullen defiance to and fro, and Mr Brownlow had sat, shading his face with his hand. "But what do you want with me?"

"You have a brother," said Mr Brownlow, rousing himself, "a brother, the whisper of whose name in your ear when I came behind you in the street, was, in itself, almost enough to make you accompany me hither, in wonder and alarm."

"I have no brother," replied Monks. "You know I was an only child. Why do you talk to me of brothers? You know that, as well as I."

"Attend to what I do know, and you may not," said Mr Brownlow. "I shall interest you by and by. I know that of the wretched marriage, into which family pride, and the most sordid and narrowest of all ambition, forced your unhappy father when a mere boy, you were the sole and most unnatural issue."

"I don't care for hard names," interrupted Monks with a jeering laugh. "You know the fact, and that's enough for me."

"But I also know," pursued the old gentleman, "the misery, the slow torture, the protracted anguish of that ill-assorted union. I know how listlessly and wearily each of that wretched pair dragged on their heavy chain through a world that was poisoned to them both. I know how cold formalities were succeeded by open taunts; how indifference gave place to dislike, dislike to hate, and hate to loathing, until at last they wrenched the clanking bond asunder, and retiring a wide space apart, carried each a galling fragment, of which nothing but death could break the rivets, to hide it in new society beneath the gayest looks they could assume. Your mother succeeded; she forgot it soon. But it rusted and cankered at your father's heart for years."

"Well, they were separated," said Monks, "and what of that?"

"When they had been separated for some time," returned Mr Brownlow, "and your mother, wholly given up to continental frivolities, had utterly forgotten the young husband ten good years her junior, who, with prospects blighted, lingered on at home, he fell among new friends. *This* circumstance, at least, you know already."

"Not I," said Monks, turning away his eyes and beating his foot upon the ground, as a man who is determined to deny everything. "Not I."

"Your manner, no less than your actions, assures me that you have never forgotten it, or ceased to think of it with bitterness," returned Mr Brownlow. "I speak of fifteen years ago, when you were not more than eleven years old, and your father but one-and-thirty – for he was, I repeat, a boy, when *his* father ordered him to marry. Must I go back to events which cast a shade upon the memory of your parent, or will you spare it, and disclose to me the truth?"

"I have nothing to disclose," rejoined Monks. "You must talk on if you will."

"These new friends, then," said Mr Brownlow, "were a naval officer retired from active service, whose wife had died some half-a-year before, and left him with two children – there had been more, but, of all their family, happily but two survived. They were both daughters; one a beautiful creature of nineteen, and the other a mere child of two or three years old."

"What's this to me?" asked Monks.

"They resided," said Mr Brownlow, without seeming to hear the interruption, "in a part of the country to which your father in his wandering had repaired, and where he had taken up his abode. Acquaintance, intimacy, friendship, fast followed on each other. Your father was gifted as few men are. He had his sister's soul and person. As the old officer knew him more and more, he grew to love him. I would that it had ended there. His daughter did the same."

The old gentleman paused; Monks was biting his lips, with his eyes fixed upon the floor; seeing this, he immediately resumed:

"The end of a year found him contracted, solemnly contracted, to that daughter; the object of the first, true, ardent, only passion of a guileless girl."

"Your tale is of the longest," observed Monks, moving restlessly in his chair.

"It is a true tale of grief and trial, and sorrow, young man," returned Mr Brownlow, "and such tales usually are; if it were one of unmixed joy and happiness, it would be very brief. At length one of those rich relations to strengthen whose interest and importance your father had been sacrificed, as others are often – it is no uncommon case – died, and to repair the misery he had been instrumental in occasioning, left him *his* panacea for all griefs – Money. It was necessary that he should immediately repair to Rome, whither this man had sped for health, and where he had died, leaving his affairs in great confusion. He went; was seized with mortal illness there; was followed, the moment the intelligence reached Paris, by your mother who carried you with her; he died the day after her arrival, leaving no will—*no will*—so that the whole property fell to her and you."

At this part of the recital Monks held his breath, and listened with a face of intense eagerness, though his eyes were not directed towards the speaker. As Mr Brownlow paused, he changed his position with the air of one who has experienced a sudden relief, and wiped his hot face and hands.

"Before he went abroad, and as he passed through London on his way," said Mr Brownlow, slowly, and fixing his eyes upon the other's face, "he came to me."

"I never heard of that," interrupted Monks in a tone intended to appear incredulous, but savouring more of disagreeable surprise.

"He came to me, and left with me, among some other things, a picture – a portrait painted by himself – a likeness of this poor girl – which he did not wish to leave behind, and could not carry forward on his hasty journey. He was worn by anxiety and remorse almost to a shadow; talked in a wild, distracted way, of ruin and dishonour worked by himself; confided to me his intention to convert his whole property, at any loss, into money, and, having settled on his wife and you a portion of his recent acquisition, to fly the country – I guessed too well he would not fly alone – and never see it more. Even from me, his old and early friend, whose strong attachment had taken root in the earth that covered one most dear to both – even from me he withheld any more particular confession, promising to write and tell me all, and after that to see me once again, for the last time on earth. Alas! *That* was the last time. I had no letter, and I never saw him more."

"I went," said Mr Brownlow, after a short pause, "I went, when all was over, to the scene of his – I will use the term the world would freely use, for worldly harshness or favour are now alike to him – of his guilty love, resolved that if my fears were realized that erring child should find one heart and home to shelter and compassionate her. The family had left that part a week before; they had called in such trifling debts as were outstanding, discharged them, and left the place by night. Why, or whither, none can tell."

Monks drew his breath yet more freely, and looked round with a smile of triumph.

"When your brother," said Mr Brownlow, drawing nearer to the other's chair, "When your brother: a feeble, ragged, neglected child: was cast in my way by a stronger hand than chance, and rescued by me from a life of vice and infamy—"

"What?" cried Monks.

"By me," said Mr Brownlow. "I told you I should interest you before long.

I say by me – I see that your cunning associate suppressed my name, although for aught he knew, it would be quite strange to your ears. When he was rescued by me, then, and lay recovering from sickness in my house, his strong resemblance to this picture I have spoken of, struck me with astonishment. Even when I first saw him in all his dirt and misery, there was a lingering expression in his face that came upon me like a glimpse of some old friend flashing on one in a vivid dream. I need not tell you he was snared away before I knew his history—"

"Why not?" asked Monks hastily.

"Because you know it well."

"I!"

"Denial to me is vain," replied Mr Brownlow. "I shall show you that I know more than that."

"You – you – can't prove anything against me," stammered Monks. "I defy you to do it!"

"We shall see," returned the old gentleman, with a searching glance. "I lost the boy, and no efforts of mine could recover him. Your mother being dead, I knew that you alone could solve the mystery if anybody could, and as when I had last heard of you you were on your own estate in the West Indies – whither, as you well know, you retired upon your mother's death to escape the consequences of vicious courses here – I made the voyage. You had left it, months before, and were supposed to be in London, but no one could tell where. I returned. Your agents had no clue to your residence. You came and went, they said, as strangely as you had ever done: sometimes for days together and sometimes not for months: keeping to all appearance the same low haunts and mingling with the same infamous herd who had been your associates when a fierce ungovernable boy. I wearied them with new applications. I paced the streets by night and day, but until two hours ago, all my efforts were fruitless, and I never saw you for an instant."

"And now you do see me," said Monks, rising boldly, "what then? Fraud and robbery are high-sounding words – justified, you think, by a fancied resemblance in some young imp to an idle daub of a dead man's. Brother! You don't even know that a child was born of this maudlin pair; you don't even know that."

"I *did not,*" replied Mr Brownlow, rising too; "but within the last fortnight I have learnt it all. You have a brother; you know it, and him. There was a will, which your mother destroyed, leaving the secret and the gain to you at her own death. It contained a reference to some child likely to be the result of this sad connection, which child was born, and accidentally encountered by you, when your suspicions were first awakened by his resemblance to his father. You repaired to the place of his birth. There existed proofs – proofs long suppressed – of his birth and parentage. Those proofs were destroyed by you, and now, in your own words to your accomplice Fagin, '*the only proofs of the boy's identity lie at the bottom of the river, and the old hag that received them from the mother is rotting in her coffin.*' Unworthy son, coward, liar – you, who hold your councils with thieves and murderers in dark rooms at night – you, whose plots and wiles have brought a violent death upon the head of one worth millions such as you – you, who from your cradle were gall and bitterness to your own father's heart, and in whom all evil passions, vice, and profligacy, festered, till they found a vent in a hideous disease which has made your face an index even to your mind – you, Edward Leeford, do you still brave me?"

"No, no, no!" returned the coward, overwhelmed by these accumulated charges.

"Every word!" cried the gentleman, "every word that has passed between you and this detested villain, is known to me. Shadows on the wall have caught your whispers, and brought them to my ear; the sight of the persecuted child has turned vice itself, and given it the courage and almost the attributes of virtue. Murder has been done, to which you were morally if not really a party."

"No, no," interposed Monks. "I – I know nothing of that; I was going to inquire the truth of the story when you overtook me. I didn't know the cause. I thought it was a common quarrel."

"It was the partial disclosure of your secrets," replied Mr Brownlow. "Will you disclose the whole?"

"Yes, I will."

"Set your hand to a statement of truth and facts, and repeat it before witnesses?"

"That I promise too."

"Remain quietly here, until such a document is drawn up, and proceed with me to such a place as I may deem most advisable, for the purpose of attesting it?"

"If you insist upon that, I'll do that also," replied Monks.

"You must do more than that," said Mr Brownlow. "Make restitution to an innocent and unoffending child, for such he is, although the offspring of a guilty and most miserable love. You have not forgotten the provisions of the will. Carry them into execution so far as your brother is concerned, and then go where you please. In this world you need meet no more."

While Monks was pacing up and down, meditating with dark and evil looks on this proposal and the possibilities of evading it: torn by his fears on the one hand and his hatred on the other: the door was hurriedly unlocked, and a gentleman (Mr Losberne) entered the room in violent agitation.

"The man will be taken," he cried. "He will be taken tonight!"

"The murderer?" asked Mr Brownlow.

"Yes, yes," replied the other. "His dog has been seen lurking about some old haunt, and there seems little doubt that his master either is, or will be, there, under cover of the darkness. Spies are hovering about in every direction. I have spoken to the men who are charged with his capture, and they tell me he cannot escape. A reward of a hundred pounds is proclaimed by Government tonight."

"I will give fifty more," said Mr Brownlow, "and proclaim it with my own lips upon the spot, if I can reach it. Fagin; what of him?"

"When I last heard, he had not been taken, but he will be, or is, by this time. They're sure of him."

"Have you made up your mind?" asked Mr Brownlow, in a low voice, of Monks.

"Yes," he replied. "You – you – will be secret with me?"

"I will. Remain here till I return. It is your only hope of safety."

They left the room, and the door was again locked.

"What have you done?" asked the doctor in a whisper.

"All that I could hope to do, and even more. Coupling the poor girl's intelligence with my previous knowledge, and the result of our good friend's inquiries on the spot, I left him no loophole of escape, and laid bare the whole villany which by these lights became plain as day. Write and appoint the evening after tomorrow, at seven, for the meeting. We shall be down there, a few hours before, but shall require rest: especially the young lady, who *may* have greater need of firmness than either you or I can quite foresee just now. But my blood boils to avenge this poor murdered creature. Which way have they taken?"

"Drive straight to the office and you will be in time," replied Mr Losberne. "I will remain here."

The two gentlemen hastily separated; each in a fever of excitement wholly uncontrollable.

CHAPTER 35

THE PURSUIT AND ESCAPE

Near to that part of the Thames on which the church at Rotherhithe abuts, where the buildings on the banks are dirtiest and the vessels on the river blackest with the dust of colliers and the smoke of close-built low-roofed houses, there exists the filthiest, the strangest, the most extraordinary of the many localities that are hidden in London, wholly unknown, even by name, to the great mass of its inhabitants.

In such a neighbourhood stands Jacob's Island, surrounded by a muddy ditch, six or eight feet deep and fifteen or twenty wide when the tide is in, known as Folly Ditch. It is a creek or inlet from the Thames, and can always be filled at high water by opening the sluices at the Lead Mills.

In Jacob's Island, the warehouses are roofless and empty; the walls are crumbling down; the windows are windows no more. The houses have no owners; they are broken open, and entered upon by those who have the courage; and there they live, and there they die. They must have powerful motives for a secret residence, or be reduced to a destitute condition indeed, who seek a refuge in Jacob's Island.

In an upper room of one of these houses – a detached house of fair size, ruinous in other respects, but strongly defended at door and window: of which house the back commanded the ditch in manner already described – there were assembled three men, who, regarding each other every now and then with looks expressive of perplexity and expectation, sat for some time in profound and gloomy silence. One of these was Toby Crackit, another Mr Chitling, and the third a robber of fifty years, whose nose had been almost beaten in, in some old scuffle, and whose face bore a frightful scar which might probably be traced to the same occasion. This man was a returned transport, and his name was Kags.

Toby Crackit, seeming to abandon as hopeless any further effort to maintain his usual devil-may-care swagger, turned to Chitling and said,

"When was Fagin took then?"

"Just at dinner-time – two o'clock this afternoon."

A pattering noise was heard upon the stairs, and Sikes's dog bounded into the room. They ran to the window, downstairs, and into the street. The dog had jumped in at an open window; he made no attempt to follow them, nor was his master to be seen.

"What's the meaning of this?" said Toby, when they had returned. "He can't be coming here. I – I – hope not."

"If he was coming here, he'd have come with the dog," said Kags, stooping down to examine the animal, who lay panting on the floor. "Here! Give us some water for him; he has run himself faint."

"He's drunk it all up, every drop," said Chitling after watching the dog some time in silence. "Covered with mud – lame – half-blind – he must have come a long way."

"Where can he have come from!" exclaimed Toby. "He's been to the other kens of course, and finding them filled with strangers come on here, where he's been many a time and often. But where can he have come from first, and how comes he here alone without the other!"

"He – " (none of them called the murderer by his old name) – "He can't have made away with himself. What do you think?" said Chitling.

Toby shook his head.

"If he had," said Kags, "the dog 'ud want to lead us away to where he did it. No. I think he's got out of the country, and left the dog behind. He must have given him the slip somehow, or he wouldn't be so easy."

This solution, appearing the most probable one, was adopted as the right; the dog, creeping under a chair, coiled himself up to sleep, without more notice from anybody.

It being now dark, the shutter was closed, and a candle lighted and placed upon the table. The terrible events of the last two days had made a deep impression on all three, increased by the danger and uncertainty of their own position. They drew their chairs closer together, starting at every sound. They spoke little, and that in whispers, and were as silent and awe-stricken as if the remains of the murdered woman lay in the next room.

They had sat thus, some time, when suddenly was heard a hurried knocking at the door below.

"Young Bates," said Kags, looking angrily round, to check the fear he felt himself.

The knocking came again. No, it wasn't he. He never knocked like that.

Crackit went to the window, and shaking all over, drew in his head. There was no need to tell them who it was; his pale face was enough. The dog too was on the alert in an instant, and ran whining to the door.

"We must let him in," he said, taking up the candle.

"Isn't there any help for it?" asked the other man in a hoarse voice.

"None. He *must* come in."

"Don't leave us in the dark," said Kags, taking down a candle from the chimney-piece, and lighting it, with such a trembling hand that the knocking was twice repeated before he had finished.

Crackit went down to the door, and returned followed by a man with the lower part of his face buried in a handkerchief, and another tied over his head under his hat. He drew them slowly off. Blanched face, sunken eyes, hollow cheeks, beard of three days' growth, wasted flesh, short thick breath; it was the very ghost of Sikes.

He laid his hand upon a chair which stood in the middle of the room, but shuddering as he was about to drop into it, and seeming to glance over his shoulder, dragged it back close to the wall – as close as it would go – ground it against it – and sat down.

Not a word had been exchanged. He looked from one to another in silence. If an eye were furtively raised and met his, it was instantly averted. When his hollow voice broke silence, they all three started. They seemed never to have heard its tones before.

"How came that dog here?" he asked.

"Alone. Three hours ago."

"Tonight's paper says that Fagin's took. Is it true, or a lie?"

"True."

They were silent again.

"Damn you all!" said Sikes, passing his hand across his forehead. "Have you nothing to say to me?"

There was an uneasy movement among them, but nobody spoke.

"You that keep this house," said Sikes, turning his face to Crackit, "do you mean to sell me, or to let me lie here till this hunt is over?"

"You may stop here, if you think it safe," returned the person addressed, after some hesitation.

Sikes carried his eyes slowly up the wall behind him: rather trying to turn his head than actually doing it: and said, "Is – it – the body – is it buried?"

They shook their heads.

"Why isn't it!" he retorted with the same glance behind him. "Wot do they keep such ugly things above the ground for? – Who's that knocking?"

Crackit intimated, by a motion of his hand as he left the room, that there was nothing to fear; and directly came back with Charley Bates behind him. Sikes sat opposite the door, so that the moment the boy entered the room he encountered his figure.

"Toby," said the boy, falling back, as Sikes turned his eyes towards him, "why didn't you tell me this, downstairs?"

There had been something so tremendous in the shrinking off of the three, that the wretched man was willing to propitiate even this lad. Accordingly he nodded, and made as though he would shake hands with him.

"Let me go into some other room," said the boy, retreating still farther.

"Charley!" said Sikes, stepping forward. "Don't you – don't you know me?"

"Don't come nearer me," answered the boy, still retreating, and looking, with horror in his eyes, upon the murderer's face. "You monster!"

The man stopped halfway, and they looked at each other; but Sikes's eyes sunk gradually to the ground.

"Witness you three," cried the boy, shaking his clenched fist, and becoming more and more excited as he spoke. "Witness you three – I'm not afraid of him – if they come here after him, I'll give him up; I will. I tell you out at once. He may kill me for it if he likes, or if he dares, but if I'm here I'll give him up. I'd give him up if he was to be boiled alive. Murder! Help! If there's the pluck of a man among you three, you'll help me. Murder! Help! Down with him!"

Pouring out these cries, and accompanying them with violent gesticulation, the boy actually threw himself, single-handed, upon the strong man, and in the intensity of his energy and the suddenness of his surprise, brought him heavily to the ground.

The three spectators seemed quite stupefied. They offered no interference, and the boy and man rolled on the ground together; the former, heedless of the blows that showered upon him, wrenching his hands tighter and tighter in the garments about the murderer's breast, and never ceasing to call for help with all his might.

The contest, however, was too unequal to last long. Sikes had him down, and his knee was on his throat, when Crackit pulled him back with a look of alarm, and pointed to the window. There were lights gleaming below, voices in loud and earnest conversation, the tramp of hurried footsteps – endless they seemed in number – crossing the nearest wooden bridge. One man on horseback seemed to be among the crowd; for there was the noise of hoofs rattling on the uneven pavement. The gleam of lights increased; the footsteps came more thickly and noisily on. Then, came a loud knocking at the door, and then a hoarse murmur from such a multitude of angry voices as would have made the boldest quail.

"Help!" shrieked the boy in a voice that rent the air. "He's here! Break down the door!"

"In the King's name," cried the voices without; and the hoarse cry arose again, but louder.

"Break down the door!" screamed the boy. "I tell you they'll never open it. Run straight to the room where the light is. Break down the door!"

Strokes, thick and heavy, rattled upon the door and lower window-shutters, as he ceased to speak, and a loud huzzah burst from the crowd; giving the listener, for the first time, some adequate idea of its immense extent.

"Open the door of some place where I can lock this screeching Hell-babe," cried Sikes fiercely; running to and fro, and dragging the boy, now, as easily as if he were an empty sack. "That door. Quick!" He flung him in, bolted it, and turned the key. "Is the downstairs door fast?"

"Double-locked and chained," replied Crackit, who, with the other two men, still remained quite helpless and bewildered.

"The panels – are they strong?"

"Lined with sheet-iron."

"And the windows too?"

"Yes, and the windows."

"Damn you!" cried the desperate ruffian, throwing up the sash and menacing the crowd. "Do your worst! I'll cheat you yet!"

Of all the terrific yells that ever fell on mortal ears, none could exceed the cry of the infuriated throng.

"The tide," cried the murderer, as he staggered back into the room, and shut the faces out, "the tide was in as I came up. Give me a rope, a long rope. They're all in front. I may drop into the Folly Ditch, and clear off that way. Give me a rope, or I shall do three more murders and kill myself."

The panic-stricken men pointed to where such articles were kept; the murderer, hastily selecting the longest and strongest cord, hurried up to the house-top.

All the windows in the rear of the house had been long ago bricked up, except one small trap in the room where the boy was locked, and that was too small even for the passage of his body. But, from this aperture, he had never ceased to call on those without, to guard the back; and thus, when the murderer emerged at last on the house-top by the door in the roof, a

loud shout proclaimed the fact to those in front, who immediately began to pour round, pressing upon each other in an unbroken stream.

He planted a board, which he had carried up with him for the purpose, so firmly against the door that it must be matter of great difficulty to open it from the inside; and creeping over the tiles, looked over the low parapet.

The water was out, and the ditch a bed of mud.

The crowd had been hushed during these few moments, watching his motions and doubtful of his purpose, but the instant they perceived it and knew it was defeated, they raised a cry of triumphant execration to which all their previous shouting had been whispers. Again and again it rose. Those who were at too great a distance to know its meaning, took up the sound; it echoed and re-echoed; it seemed as though the whole city had poured its population out to curse him.

"They have him now," cried a man on the nearest bridge. "Hurrah!"

The crowd grew light with uncovered heads; and again the shout uprose.

"I will give fifty pounds," cried an old gentleman from the same quarter, "to the man who takes him alive. I will remain here, till he comes to ask me for it."

The man had shrunk down, thoroughly quelled by the ferocity of the crowd, and the impossibility of escape; he sprang upon his feet, determined to make one last effort for his life by dropping into the ditch, and, at the risk of being stifled, endeavouring to creep away in the darkness and confusion.

Roused into new strength and energy, and stimulated by the noise within the house which announced that an entrance had really been effected, he set his foot against the stack of chimneys, fastened one end of the rope tightly and firmly round it, and with the other made a strong running noose by the aid of his hands and teeth almost in a second. He could let himself down by the cord to within a less distance of the ground than his own height, and had his knife ready in his hand to cut it then and drop.

At the very instant when he brought the loop over his head previous to slipping it beneath his armpits, and when the old gentleman before-mentioned (who had clung so tight to the railing of the bridge as to resist the force of the crowd, and retain his position) earnestly warned those about him that the man was about to lower himself down – at that very instant the murderer, looking behind him on the roof, threw his arms above his head, and uttered a yell of terror.

"The eyes again!" he cried in an unearthly screech.

Staggering as if struck by lightning, he lost his balance and tumbled over the parapet. The noose was on his neck. It ran up with his weight, tight as a bowstring, and swift as the arrow it speeds. He fell for five-and-thirty feet. There was a sudden jerk, a terrific convulsion of the limbs; and there he hung, with the open knife clenched in his stiffening hand.

The old chimney quivered with the shock, but stood it bravely. The murderer swung lifeless against the wall; and the boy, thrusting aside the dangling body which obscured his view, called to the people to come and take him out, for God's sake.

A dog, which had lain concealed till now, ran backwards and forwards on the parapet with a dismal howl, and collecting himself for a spring, jumped for the dead man's shoulders. Missing his aim, he fell into the ditch, turning completely over as he went; and striking his head against a stone, dashed out his brains.

CHAPTER 36

AFFORDING AN EXPLANATION OF MORE MYSTERIES THAN ONE

The events narrated in the last chapter were yet but two days old, when Oliver found himself, at three o'clock in the afternoon, in a travelling-carriage rolling fast towards his native town. Mrs Maylie, and Rose, and Mrs Bedwin, and the good doctor were with him: and Mr Brownlow followed in a post-chaise, accompanied by one other person whose name had not been mentioned.

As they approached the town, and at length drove through its narrow streets, it became matter of no small difficulty to restrain the boy within reasonable bounds. There was Sowerberry's the undertaker's just as it used to be, only smaller and less imposing in appearance than he remembered it – there were all the well-known shops and houses, with almost every one of which he had some slight incident connected.

They drove straight to the door of the chief hotel (which Oliver used to stare up at, with awe, and think a mighty palace, but which had somehow fallen off in grandeur and size); and here was Mr Grimwig all ready to receive them. There was dinner prepared, and there were bedrooms ready, and everything was arranged as if by magic.

Notwithstanding all this, when the hurry of the first half-hour was over, the same silence and constraint prevailed that had marked their journey down. Mr Brownlow did not join them at dinner, but remained in a separate room.

At length, when nine o'clock had come, and they began to think they were to hear no more that night, Mr Losberne and Mr Grimwig entered the room, followed by Mr Brownlow and a man whom Oliver almost shrieked with surprise to see; for they told him it was his brother. Monks cast a look of hate, which, even then, he could not dissemble, at the astonished boy, and sat down near the door. Mr Brownlow, who had papers in his hand, walked to a table near which Rose and Oliver were seated.

"This is a painful task," said he, "but these declarations, which have been signed in London before many gentlemen, must be in substance repeated here. I would have spared you the degradation, but we must hear them from your own lips before we part, and you know why."

"Go on," said the person addressed, turning away his face. "Quick. I have almost done enough, I think. Don't keep me here."

"This child," said Mr Brownlow, drawing Oliver to him, and laying his hand upon his head, "is your half-brother; the illegitimate son of your father, my dear friend Edwin Leeford, by poor young Agnes Fleming, who died in giving him birth."

"Yes," said Monks, scowling at the trembling boy: the beating of whose heart he might have heard. "That is their bastard child."

"The term you use," said Mr Brownlow sternly, "is a reproach to those who long since passed beyond the feeble censure of the world. It reflects disgrace on no one living, except you who use it. Let that pass. He was born in this town?"

"In the workhouse of this town," was the sullen reply. "You have the story there." He pointed impatiently to the papers as he spoke.

"I must have it here, too," said Mr Brownlow, looking round upon the listeners.

"Listen then! You!" returned Monks. "His father being taken ill at Rome, was joined by his wife, my mother, from whom he had been long separated, who went from Paris and took me with her – to look after his property, for what I know, for she had no great affection for him, nor he for her. He knew nothing of us, for his senses were gone, and he slumbered on till next day, when he died. Among the papers in his desk, were two, dated on the night his illness first came on, directed to yourself"; he addressed himself to Mr Brownlow; "and enclosed in a few short lines to you, with an intimation on the cover of the package that it was not to be forwarded till after he was dead. One of these papers was a letter to this girl Agnes; the other a will."

"What of the letter?" asked Mr Brownlow.

"The letter? – A sheet of paper crossed and crossed again with a penitent confession, and prayers to God to help her. He had palmed a tale on the girl that some secret mystery – to be explained one day – prevented his marrying her just then; and so she had gone on, trusting patiently to him, until she trusted too far, and lost what none could ever give her back. She was, at that time, within a few months of her confinement. He told her all he had meant to do, to hide her shame, if he had lived, and prayed her, if he died, not to curse his memory, or think the consequences of their sin would be visited on her or their young child; for all the guilt was his. He reminded her of the day he had given her the little locket and the ring with her christian name engraved upon it, and a blank left for that which he hoped one day to have bestowed upon her – prayed her yet to keep it, and wear it next her heart, as she had done before – and then ran on, wildly, in the same words, over and over again, as if he had gone distracted. I believe he had."

"The will," said Mr Brownlow, as Oliver's tears fell fast.

Monks was silent.

"The will," said Mr Brownlow, speaking for him, "was in the same spirit as the letter. He talked of miseries which his wife had brought upon him; of the rebellious disposition, vice, malice, and premature bad passions of you his only son, who had been trained to hate him; and left you, and your mother, each an annuity of eight hundred pounds. The bulk of his property he divided into two equal portions – one for Agnes Fleming, and the other for their child, if it should be born alive, and ever come of age. If it were a girl, it was to inherit the money unconditionally; but if a boy, only on the stipulation that in his minority he should never have stained his name with any public act of dishonour, meanness, cowardice, or wrong. He did this, he said, to mark his confidence in the mother, and his conviction – only strengthened by approaching death – that the child would share her gentle heart, and noble nature. If he were disappointed in this expectation, then the money was to come to you: for then, and not till then, when both children were equal, would he recognize your prior claim upon his purse, who had none upon his heart, but had, from an infant, repulsed him with coldness and aversion."

"My mother," said Monks, in a louder tone, "did what a woman should have done. She burnt this will. The letter never reached its destination; but that, and other proofs, she kept, in case they ever tried to lie away the blot. The girl's father had the truth from her with every aggravation that her violent hate – I love her for it now – could add. Goaded by shame and dishonour he fled with his children into a remote corner of Wales,

changing his very name that his friends might never know of his retreat; and here, no great while afterwards, he was found dead in his bed. The girl had left her home, in secret, some weeks before; he had searched for her, on foot, in every town and village near; it was on the night when he returned home, assured that she had destroyed herself, to hide her shame and his, that his old heart broke."

There was a short silence here, until Mr Brownlow took up the thread of the narrative.

"Years after this," he said, "this man's – Edward Leeford's – mother came to me. He had left her, when only eighteen; robbed her of jewels and money; gambled, squandered, forged, and fled to London: where for

two years he had associated with the lowest outcasts. She was sinking under a painful and incurable disease, and wished to recover him before she died. Inquiries were set on foot, and strict searches made. They were unavailing for a long time, but ultimately successful; and he went back with her to France."

"There she died," said Monks, "after a lingering illness; and, on her death-bed, she bequeathed these secrets to me, together with her unquenchable and deadly hatred of all whom they involved – though she need not have left me that, for I had inherited it long before. She would not believe that the girl had destroyed herself, and the child too, but was filled with the impression that a male child had been born, and was alive.

I swore to her, if ever it crossed my path, to hunt it down; never to let it rest; to pursue it with the bitterest and most unrelenting animosity; to vent upon it the hatred that I deeply felt, and to spit upon the empty vaunt of that insulting will by dragging it, if I could, to the very gallows-foot. She was right. He came in my way at last. I began well; and, but for babbling drabs, I would have finished as I began!"

As the villain folded his arms tight together, and muttered curses on himself in the impotence of baffled malice, Mr Brownlow turned to the terrified group beside him, and explained that Fagin, who had been his old accomplice and confidant, had a large reward for keeping Oliver ensnared: of which some part was to be given up, in the event of his being rescued.

"The locket and ring?" said Mr Brownlow, turning to Monks.

"I bought them from the man and woman I told you of, who stole them from the nurse, who stole them from the corpse," answered Monks without raising his eyes. "You know what became of them."

Mr Brownlow merely nodded to Mr Grimwig, who, disappearing with great alacrity, shortly returned, pushing in Mrs Bumble, and dragging her unwilling consort after him.

"Do my hi's deceive me!" cried Mr Bumble, with ill-feigned enthusiasm, "or is that little Oliver? Oh O-li-ver, if you know'd how I've been a-grieving for you—"

"Hold your tongue, fool," murmured Mrs Bumble.

"Isn't natur, natur, Mrs Bumble?" remonstrated the workhouse master. "Can't I be supposed to feel – *I* as brought him up porochially – when I see him a-setting here among ladies and gentlemen of the very affablest description! I always loved that boy as if he'd been my – my – my own grandfather," said Mr Bumble, halting for an appropriate comparison.

"Master Oliver, my dear, you remember the blessed gentleman in the white waistcoat? Ah! he went to heaven last week, in a oak coffin with plated handles, Oliver."

"Come, sir," said Mr Grimwig, tartly; "suppress your feelings."

"I will do my endeavours, sir," replied Mr Bumble. "How do you do, sir? I hope you are very well."

This salutation was addressed to Mr Brownlow, who had stepped up to within a short distance of the respectable couple. He inquired, as he pointed to Monks,

"Do you know that person?"

"No," replied Mrs Bumble flatly.

"Perhaps *you* don't?" said Mr Brownlow, addressing her spouse.

"I never saw him in all my life," said Mr Bumble.

"Nor sold him anything, perhaps?"

"No," replied Mrs Bumble.

"You never had, perhaps, a certain gold locket and ring?" said Mr Brownlow.

"Certainly not," replied the matron. "Why are we brought here to answer to such nonsense as this?"

Again Mr Brownlow nodded to Mr Grimwig; and again that gentleman limped away with extraordinary readiness. But not again did he return with a stout man and wife; for this time, he led in two palsied women, who shook and tottered as they walked.

"You shut the door the night old Sally died," said the foremost one, raising her shrivelled hand, "but you couldn't shut out the sound, nor stop the chinks."

"No, no," said the other, looking round her and wagging her toothless jaws. "No, no, no."

"We heard her try to tell you what she'd done, and saw you take a paper from her hand, and watched you too, next day, to the pawnbroker's shop," said the first.

"Yes," added the second, "and it was a 'locket and gold ring.' We found out that, and saw it given you. We were by. Oh! we were by."

"And we know more than that," resumed the first, "for she told us often, long ago, that the young mother had told her that, feeling she should never get over it, she was on her way, at the time that she was taken ill, to die near the grave of the father of the child."

"Would you like to see the pawnbroker himself?" asked Mr Grimwig with a motion towards the door.

"No," replied the woman; "if he" – she pointed to Monks – "has been coward enough to confess, as I see he has, and you have sounded all these hags till you have found the right ones, I have nothing more to say. I *did* sell them, and they're where you'll never get them. What then?"

"Nothing," replied Mr Brownlow, "except that it remains for us to take care that neither of you is employed in a situation of trust again. You may leave the room."

"I hope," said Mr Bumble, looking about him with great ruefulness, as Mr Grimwig disappeared with the two old women: "I hope that this unfortunate little circumstance will not deprive me of my porochial office?"

"Indeed it will," replied Mr Brownlow. "You may make up your mind to that, and think yourself well off besides."

"It was all Mrs Bumble. She *would* do it," urged Mr Bumble; first looking round to ascertain that his partner had left the room.

"That is no excuse," replied Mr Brownlow. "You were present on the occasion of the destruction of these trinkets, and indeed are the more guilty of the two, in the eye of the law; for the law supposes that your wife acts under your direction."

"If the law supposes that," said Mr Bumble, squeezing his hat emphatically in both hands, "the law is a ass – a idiot. If that's the eye of the law, the law is a bachelor; and the worst I wish the law is, that his eye may be opened by experience – by experience."

Laying great stress on the repetition of these two words, Mr Bumble fixed his hat on very tight, and putting his hands in his pockets, followed his helpmate downstairs.

"Young lady," said Mr Brownlow, turning to Rose, "give me your hand. Do not tremble. You need not fear to hear the few remaining words we have to say."

"If they have – I do not know how they can, but if they have – any reference to me," said Rose, "pray let me hear them at some other time. I have not strength or spirits now."

"Nay," returned the old gentlman, drawing her arm through his; "you have more fortitude than this, I am sure. Do you know this young lady, sir?"

"Yes," replied Monks.

"I never saw you before," said Rose faintly.

"I have seen you often," returned Monks.

"The father of the unhappy Agnes had *two* daughters," said Mr Brownlow. "What was the fate of the other – the child?"

"The child," replied Monks, "when her father died in a strange place, in a strange name, without a letter, book, or scrap of paper that yielded the faintest clue by which his friends or relatives could be traced – the child was taken by some wretched cottagers, who reared it as their own."

"Go on," said Mr Brownlow, signing to Mrs Maylie to approach. "Go on!"

"You couldn't find the spot to which these people had repaired," said Monks, "but where friendship fails, hatred will often force a way. My mother found it, after a year of cunning search – ay, and found the child."

"She took it, did she?"

"No. The people were poor and began to sicken – at least the man did – of their fine humanity; so she left it with them, giving them a small present of money which would not last long, and promised more, which she never meant to send. She didn't quite rely, however, on their discontent and poverty for the child's unhappiness, but told the history of the sister's shame, with such alterations as suited her; bade them take good heed of the child, for she came of bad blood; and told them she was illegitimate, and sure to go wrong at one time or other. The circumstances countenanced all this; the people believed it; and there the child dragged on an existence, miserable enough even to satisfy us, until a widow lady, residing, then, at Chester, saw the girl by chance, pitied her, and took her home. There was some cursed spell, I think, against us; for in spite of all our efforts she remained there and was happy. I lost sight of her, two or three years ago, and saw her no more until a few months back."

"Do you see her now?"

"Yes. Leaning on your arm."

"But not the less my niece," cried Mrs Maylie, folding the fainting girl in her arms; "not the less my dearest child. I would not lose her now, for all the treasures of the world. My sweet companion, my own dear girl!"

"The only friend I ever had," cried Rose, clinging to her. "The kindest, best of friends. My heart will burst. I cannot bear all this."

"You have borne more, and have been, through all, the best and gentlest creature that ever shed happiness on every one she knew," said Mrs Maylie, embracing her tenderly. "Come, come, my love, remember who this is who waits to clasp you in his arms, poor child! See here – look, look, my dear!"

"Not aunt," cried Oliver, throwing his arms about her neck; "I'll never call her aunt – sister, my own dear sister, that something taught my heart to love so dearly from the first! Rose, dear, darling Rose!"

Let the tears which fell, and the broken words which were exchanged in the long close embrace between the orphans, be sacred. A father, sister, and mother, were gained, and lost, in that one moment. Joy and grief were mingled in the cup; but there were no bitter tears: for even grief itself arose so softened, and clothed in such sweet and tender recollections, that it became a solemn pleasure, and lost all character of pain.

CHAPTER 37

FAGIN'S LAST NIGHT ALIVE

The court was paved, from floor to roof, with human faces. Inquisitive and eager eyes peered from every inch of space. From the rail before the dock, away into the sharpest angle of the smallest corner in the galleries, all looks were fixed upon one man – Fagin. Before him and behind: above, below, on the right and on the left: he seemed to stand surrounded by a firmament, all bright with gleaming eyes.

A slight bustle in the court recalled him to himself. Looking round, he saw that the jurymen had turned together, to consider their verdict.

As he saw all this in one bewildered glance, the deathlike stillness came again, and looking back, he saw that the jurymen had turned towards the judge. Hush!

They only sought permission to retire.

He looked, wistfully, into their faces, one by one when they passed out, as though to see which way the greater number leant; but that was fruitless. The jailer touched him on the shoulder. He followed mechanically to the end of the dock, and sat down on a chair. The man pointed it out, or he would not have seen it.

He looked up into the gallery again. Some of the people were eating, and some fanning themselves with handkerchiefs; for the crowded place was very hot. There was one young man sketching his face in a little notebook. He wondered whether it was like, and looked on when the artist broke his pencil-point, and made another with his knife, as any idle spectator might have done.

At length there was a cry of silence, and a breathless look from all towards the door. The jury returned, and passed him close. He could glean nothing from their faces; they might as well have been of stone. Perfect stillness ensued – not a rustle – not a breath – Guilty.

They led him through a paved room under the court, where some prisoners were waiting till their turns came, and others were talking to their friends, who crowded round a grate which looked into the open yard. There was nobody there to speak to *him*; but, as he passed, the prisoners fell back to render him more visible to the people who were clinging to the bars: and they assailed him with opprobrious names, and screeched and hissed. He shook his fist, and would have spat upon them; but his conductors hurried him on, through a gloomy passage lighted by a few dim lamps, into the interior of the prison.

Here, he was searched, that he might not have about him the means of anticipating the law; this ceremony performed, they led him to one of the condemned cells, and left him there – alone.

He sat down on a stone bench opposite the door, which served for seat and bedstead; and casting his bloodshot eyes upon the ground, tried to collect his thoughts. After a while, he began to remember a few disjointed fragments of what the judge had said: though it had seemed to him, at the time, that he could not hear a word. These gradually fell into their proper places, and by degrees suggested more: so that in a little time he had the whole, almost as it was delivered. To be hanged by the neck, till he was dead – that was the end. To be hanged by the neck till he was dead.

As it came on very dark, he began to think of all the men he had known who had died upon the scaffold; some of them through his means. They rose up, in such quick succession, that he could hardly count them. He had seen some of them die – and had joked too, because they died with prayers upon their lips. With what a rattling noise the drop went down; and how suddenly they changed, from strong and vigorous men to dangling heaps of clothes!

At length, when his hands were raw with beating against the heavy door and walls, two men appeared: one bearing a candle, which he thrust into an iron candlestick fixed against the wall: the other dragging in a mattress on which to pass the night; for the prisoner was to be left alone no more.

Saturday night. He had only one night more to live. And as he thought of this, the day broke – Sunday.

He cowered down upon his stone bed, and thought of the past. He had been wounded with some missiles from the crowd on the day of his capture, and his head was bandaged with a linen cloth. His red hair hung down upon his bloodless face; his beard was torn, and twisted into knots; his eyes shone with a terrible light; his unwashed flesh crackled with the fever that burnt him up. Eight – nine – ten. If it was not a trick to frighten him, and those were the real hours treading on each other's heels, where would he be, when they came round again! Eleven! Another struck, before the voice of the previous hour had ceased to vibrate. At eight, he would be the only mourner in his own funeral train; at eleven—

The space before the prison was cleared, and a few strong barriers, painted black, had been already thrown across the road to break the pressure of the expected crowd, when Mr Brownlow and Oliver appeared at the wicket, and presented an order of admission to the prisoner, signed by one of the sheriffs. They were immediately admitted into the lodge.

"Is the young gentleman to come too, sir?" said the man whose duty it was to conduct them. "It's not a sight for children, sir."

"It is not indeed, my friend," rejoined Mr Brownlow; "but my business with this man is intimately connected with him; and as this child has seen him in the full career of his success and villany, I think it as well – even at the cost of some pain and fear – that he should see him now."

The condemned criminal was seated on his bed, rocking himself from side to side, with a countenance more like that of a snared beast than the face of a man. His mind was evidently wandering to his old life, for he continued to mutter, without appearing conscious of their presence otherwise than as a part of his vision.

"Fagin," said the jailer.

"That's me!" cried the old man, falling instantly, into the attitude of listening he had assumed upon his trial. "An old man, my Lord; a very old, old man!"

"Here," said the turnkey, laying his hand upon his breast to keep him down. "Here's somebody wants to see you, to ask you some questions, I suppose. Fagin, Fagin! Are you a man?"

"I shan't be one long," he replied, looking up with a face retaining no human expression but rage and terror. "Strike them all dead! What right have they to butcher me?"

As he spoke he caught sight of Oliver and Mr Brownlow. Shrinking to the furthest corner of the seat, he demanded to know what they wanted there.

"Steady," said the turnkey, still holding him down. "Now, sir, tell him what you want. Quick, if you please, for he grows worse as the time gets on."

"You have some papers," said Mr Brownlow advancing, "which were placed in your hands, for better security, by a man called Monks."

"It's all a lie together," replied Fagin. "I haven't one – not one."

"For the love of God," said Mr Brownlow solemnly, "do not say that now, upon the very verge of death; but tell me where they are. You know that Sikes is dead; that Monks has confessed; that there is no hope of any further gain. Where are those papers?"

"Oliver," cried Fagin, beckoning to him. "Here, here! Let me whisper to you."

"I am not afraid," said Oliver in a low voice, as he relinquished Mr Brownlow's hand.

"The papers," said Fagin, drawing Oliver towards him, "are in a canvas bag, in a hole a little way up the chimney in the top front-room. I want to talk to you, my dear. I want to talk to you."

"Yes, yes," returned Oliver. "Let me say a prayer. Do! Let me say one prayer. Say only one, upon your knees, with me, and we will talk till morning."

"Outside, outside," replied Fagin, pushing the boy before him towards the door, and looking vacantly over his head. "Say I've gone to sleep – they'll believe *you*. You can get me out, if you take me so. Now then, now then!"

"Oh! God forgive this wretched man!" cried the boy with a burst of tears.

"That's right, that's right," said Fagin. "That'll help us on. This door first. If I shake and tremble, as we pass the gallows, don't you mind, but hurry on. Now, now, now!"

"Have you nothing else to ask him, sir?" inquired the turnkey.

"No other question," replied Mr Brownlow. "If I hoped we could recall him to a sense of his position—"

"Nothing will do that, sir," replied the man, shaking his head. "You had better leave him."

The door of the cell opened, and the attendants returned.

"Press on, press on," cried Fagin. "Softly, but not so slow. Faster, faster!"

The men laid hands upon him, and disengaging Oliver from his grasp, held him back. He struggled with the power of desperation, for an instant; and then sent up cry upon cry that penetrated even those massive walls, and rang in their ears until they reached the open yard.

It was some time before they left the prison. Oliver nearly swooned after this frightful scene, and was so weak that for an hour or more, he had not the strength to walk.

Day was dawning when they again emerged. A great multitude had already assembled; the windows were filled with people, smoking and playing cards to beguile the time; the crowd were pushing, quarrelling, joking. Everything told of life and animation, but one dark cluster of objects in the centre of all – the black stage, the cross-beam, the rope, and all the hideous apparatus of death.

CHAPTER 38

AND LAST

The fortunes of those who have figured in this tale are nearly closed. The little that remains to their historian to relate, is told in few and simple words.

Monks, after undergoing a long confinement for some fresh act of fraud and knavery, at length sunk under an attack of his old disorder, and died in prison. As far from home, died the chief remaining members of his friend Fagin's gang.

Mr Brownlow adopted Oliver as his son. Removing with him and the old housekeeper to within a mile of where his dear friends resided, he gratified the only remaining wish of Oliver's warm and earnest heart, and thus linked together a little society, whose condition approached as nearly to one of perfect happiness as can ever be known in this changing world.

The worthy doctor returned to Chertsey. Before his removal, he had managed to contract a strong friendship for Mr Grimwig, which that eccentric gentleman cordially reciprocated.

Mr and Mrs Bumble, deprived of their situations, were gradually reduced to great indigence and misery, and finally became paupers in that very same workhouse in which they had once lorded it over others.

AGNES

Mr Bumble has been heard to say, that in this reverse and degradation, he has not even spirits to be thankful for being separated from his wife.

Master Charles Bates, appalled by Sikes's crime, turned his back upon the scenes of the past. He struggled hard and suffered much, but, having a contented disposition, succeeded in the end; he is now the merriest young grazier in all Northamptonshire.

And now, the hand that traces these words, falters, as it approaches the conclusion of its task.

I would fain linger yet with a few of those among whom I have so long moved, and share their happiness by endeavouring to depict it. I would show Rose Maylie in all the bloom and grace of early womanhood. I would paint her and her dead sister's child happy in their love for one another.

How Mr Brownlow went on, filling the mind of his adopted child with stores of knowledge, and becoming attached to him as his nature developed itself, and showed the thriving seeds of all he wished him to become. How the two orphans, tried by adversity, remembered its lessons in mercy to others, and mutual love – these are all matters which need not to be told. I have said that they were truly happy.

Within the altar of the old village church there stands a white marble tablet, which bears as yet but one word: "AGNES." There is no coffin in that tomb; and may it be many, many years, before another name is placed above it! But, if the spirits of the Dead ever come back to earth, to visit spots hallowed by the love – the love beyond the grave – of those whom they knew in life, I believe that the shade of Agnes sometimes hovers round that solemn nook. I believe it none the less because that nook is in a Church, and she was weak and erring.

THE END

This edition first published 2011 by Walker Books Ltd
87 Vauxhall Walk, London SE11 5HJ

2 4 6 8 10 9 7 5 3 1

This book has been typeset in Palatino

Printed in China

British Library Cataloguing in Publication Data:
a catalogue record for this book is available from the British Library

ISBN 978-1-84428-068-1

www.walker.co.uk